Silence Once Begun

Silence Once Begun

Jesse Ball

 PANTHEON BOOKS, NEW YORK

Copyright © 2014 by Jesse Ball

All rights reserved. Published in the United States by Pantheon Books, a division of Random House LLC, New York, and in Canada by Random House of Canada Limited, Toronto, Penguin Random House Companies.

Pantheon Books and colophon are registered trademarks of Random House LLC.

A portion of this work first appeared in *Printers Row Journal* in the *Chicago Tribune* (January 26, 2013).

Library of Congress Cataloging-in-Publication Data
Ball, Jesse.
  Silence once begun / Jesse Ball.
     pages cm
  ISBN 978-0-307-90848-3
  1. Journalists—Fiction.   2. Americans—Japan—Fiction.
3. Secrets—Fiction.   4. Murder—Investigation—Fiction.
I. Title.
  PS3602.A596S55 2013 813'.6—dc23   2013005948

www.pantheonbooks.com

Jacket design by Peter Mendelsund

Printed in the United States of America
First Edition
9 8 7 6 5 4 3 2 1

For K. Abe & S. Endo

The following work of fiction is partially based on fact.

Prefatory Material

A strange thing happened to me, to me and to the woman with whom I was living. We were in the midst of a fine life. I would look out ahead and I could see how shining, how beautiful the world was and would be. I had let go of many fears, concerns, worries. I felt many matters had been solved. We lived in a house with our daughter, we had been married for several years, and the life was so glad and bright, I can't tell you. I can say it, but you don't know, or I don't know how to say it correctly. There was a garden before our house with a high gate and trellis all around. We would sit there in the garden and there was time enough for everything, for anything at all. I wish for you to guess and feel the light, as if in morning, on your eyelids.

Something happened, however, something I did not foresee. She fell silent, simply stopped wanting to speak, and that life came to an end. I clung to it, though it was gone, and sought after all understanding that could be had of silence, of who becomes silent and why. Yet it was finished. I had to begin anew, and that beginning lay in trying to understand what had happened. Of course, such things aren't easy. No one can simply tell you what it is you don't understand, not with a matter as strange as that.

So, I began to seek after all such occurrences. I traveled to places, spoke to people; again and again I found myself without a way forward. I wanted to know how to avoid the unforeseeable troubles that come. Of course, it was silly. They can't be avoided. It is their nature. But, in my seeking, I found out about the matter of Oda Sotatsu. That led to the book you now hold in your hands. I am glad to present it to you, and I hope that it may do some good.

+

An incident occurred in a village near Sakai in Osaka Prefecture. I call it an incident because it is so singular. At the same time, as you will see, there are elements that make it common to all who share our human life. When I read of it, many years after it had happened, I traveled there to unearth what more I could and discover the full story.

Most of the principals were still living, and over a series of interviews, I gathered the material that now allows me to relate this tale. The names of the individuals involved have been changed to protect their identities and the identities of their loved ones and descendants. Dates, as well as particular periods of time, have also been altered as a further protection.

++

In the pages that follow this, I may occasionally refer to myself as Int. or Interviewer, or may give a note to elucidate some situation. However, most of the book's text is drawn from interviews recorded via tape-device. The book is in four accounts: the first from various people connected with (2) Oda Sotatsu, including family members and members of the metropolitan (Sakai) and local police; the second of my search for Jito Joo; the third from (3) Jito Joo; and the fourth from (1) Sato Kakuzo.

The first two sections are by necessity a narrative, with the data bound together and expressed in an at times novelistic fashion (although trouble has been taken to indicate sources). The latter sections for the most part do not necessitate this failing, as the materials alone proved sufficient to my task.

—Jesse Ball, Chicago, 2012

1__

The Situation of Oda Sotatsu

A First Telling of the Story

Oda Sotatsu was a young man in October of 1977. He was in the twenty-ninth year of his life. He worked in an office, an import/export business owned by his uncle. They principally sold thread. To do this, they bought thread also. Mostly for Sotatsu it was buying and selling thread. He did not like it very much, but went about it without complaint. He lived alone, had no girlfriend, no pets. He had a basic education and a small circle of acquaintances. He appears to have been well thought of. He liked jazz and had a record player. He wore simple, muted clothing, ate most meals at home. The more passionately he felt about a subject, the less likely he would be to join a discussion. Many people knew him, and lived beside him, near him—but few could say they had any sense of what he was really like. They had not suspected that he was really like anything. It seemed he merely was what he did: a quiet daily routine of work and sleep.

The story of Oda Sotatsu begins with a confession that he signed.

He had fallen in with a man named Kakuzo and a girl named Jito Joo. These were somewhat wild characters, particularly Sato Kakuzo. He was in trouble, or had been. People knew it.

Now this is what happened: somehow Kakuzo met Oda Sotatsu, and somehow he convinced him to sign a confession for a crime that he had not committed.

That he should sign a confession for a crime that he did not commit is strange. It is hard to believe. Yet, he did in fact sign it. When I learned of these events, and when I researched them, I found that there was a reason he did so, and that reason is—he was compelled to by a wager.

There were several accounts of how that evening went. One was the version that had been in the newspapers. Another was a version told by Oda Sotatsu's family. Still a third was the version held to by Sato Kakuzo. This final version is stronger than the others for the reason that Kakuzo taped the proceedings and showed the tape to me. I have listened to it many times, and each time, I hear things that I have not heard before. One has the impression that one can know life, actual life, from its simulacrums by the fact that actual life constantly deceives and reveals, and is consistent in doing so.

I will describe for you the events of that evening.

The Wager

When I listened to the tape, the conversation was, in places, difficult to make out. The music was loud. As the night wore on, the party drank and spoke quite rapidly. In general, the atmosphere was that of a bar. Someone (Joo?) repeatedly gets up, leaves, returns, scraping her chair loudly against the wooden floor. They spoke inconsequentially for about forty minutes, and then they reached the matter of the wager.

Kakuzo led into it quietly. He spoke fluidly and described a sort of comradeship that they shared, the three of them. He acted as though they were all fed up with life. Joo and he, he said, had been doing things to try to escape this feeling. One of those things was to wager on cards, in a private game between the two of them. He said when he would lose, he would cut himself. Or Joo would cut herself, if she should lose. He said they went from that to other things, to forcing each other to do things, in order to feel alive again. But it all revolved around the wagering, around letting life hang in a balance. Did Sotatsu not think that was fascinating? Was he in no way stirred to try it?

All night, they were at him, Joo and Kakuzo, and finally, they convinced him. In fact, they had chosen him because he had appeared to them as someone who might be convinced, who could be convinced of such a thing. And indeed, it proved true; they were able to make him join their game.

He and Kakuzo made a wager. The wager was that the loser, whoever he was, would sign a confession. Kakuzo had brought the confession. He set it out on the table. The loser would sign it, and Joo would bring it to the police station. All that one could feel in life would be gathered up into this single moment when the

6

wager went forward and one's entire life hung on the flip of a card. Kakuzo had brought the cards as well, and they sat there on the table beside the confession.

The music in the bar was loud. Oda Sotatsu's life was difficult and had not yielded to him the things he had hoped for. He liked and respected both Kakuzo and Joo and they were bent entirely on him, and on his doing of this thing.

This is how it turned out: Oda Sotatsu wagered with Sato Kakuzo. He lost the wager. He took a pen and he signed the confession, there on the table. Joo took it with her and she and Kakuzo left the bar. Oda went home to his small apartment. Whether he slept or not, we do not know.

According to His Landlady, the Next Morning

everyone in Oda Sotatsu's building woke up to a forceful knocking on the door of Oda Sotatsu's apartment. When he did not get to the door quickly enough, the door was broken down. When he did not get onto the ground quickly enough, he was thrown to the ground. Handcuffed and in great distress, he was removed and taken to a van. A witness I spoke to said he did not struggle or declare his innocence. He merely went along quietly. The landlady recalls that he was not wearing a jacket.

The Daughter of Oda's Landlady

related to me:

—You can know nothing about Oda if you do not know how kind he was and how the kindness that he was and had was in his body, really. It was not a thing of thinking or deciding. He was simply kind and did the right things many times. To show you how—I was not old enough, but my mother, she told me that when the woman who lived above him, an old woman, and he was young, Oda, maybe in his early twenties, this old woman she had some kind of furniture moved into her house. The furniture was too large for the door and it got stuck in the door and the movers had to do something with it. It was late in the day. The workday was finished. They would come back in the morning. But the old lady, she could not go in or out. She was very concerned. She was there by the door trying to peer out through whatever little holes were left. She kept saying things, all kinds of things, but the workmen had already gone. So, Oda, what does he do? He goes up there with a little lamp and he sits on one side of the door and he talks to the old woman the whole night, doesn't leave until the morning. You know, I don't think he even liked her. He was just that way. A kind boy. Matter of fact, no one liked that old woman.

Int. Note

I am trying to relate to you a tragedy. I am attempting to do so in the manner least prejudicial to the people involved, those people who were survivors of the tragedy, but also the agents of it.

Oda Sotatsu signed a confession. He did not clearly understand what he was doing, perhaps. Or perhaps he did. Nonetheless, he signed it. The next day, Saturday the fifteenth, he was dragged off to jail. Because of the comprehensive nature of the document, the confession, his guilt was never in any doubt. The trial, when it happened, was a rapid affair in which Oda Sotatsu did little, certainly nothing on his own behalf. The police attempted, over the course of the time he was in jail awaiting trial, and the time when he was on death row thereafter, to get him to speak about the crimes he had confessed. He would not. He carried a sort of tent of silence with him, and out of it he refused to come.

Oda was visited many times during the next months by Joo. He never saw Kakuzo again.

Our story continues with information related to me by officers, guards, priests, journalists (present at the time), and by the Oda family. This is how Oda Sotatsu's story is told.

SEVEN MONTHS OF CONFINEMENT

Awaiting Trial

Interrogation 1

Fifteenth of October, 1977. Oda Sotatsu brought in on suspicion of participation in the Narito Disappearances. This suspicion having to do with the confession signed by Oda, submitted to the police force anonymously. Conversation conducted in a room of the local police station. Inspector Nagano and another inspector, name unrecorded.

[*Int. note.* Transcript of session recording, possibly altered or shoddily made. Original recording not heard.]

≡

OFFICER 1   Mr. Oda. I assume you know why you are here. I assume you know why we took the trouble to bring you here, and I assume you know what the penalties are for lying to us.

OFFICER 2   Mr. Oda, if you have any information about the whereabouts of the individuals mentioned in your confession, or if you know any of them to still be living, tell us now. It could help your case greatly, such information.

OFFICER 1   We have read your confession. We are very interested in obtaining more information pertaining to it as soon as possible.

ODA   (silent)

OFFICER 1   Mr. Oda, your predicament is not enviable. I can assure you, it is almost certain that if you are convicted you will be taken to an execution room in X. prison and hanged. If any of the individuals mentioned in your confession are still living, and you cooperate with us to find them, it could help you. It could make the difference. You could live.

ODA   (silent)

OFFICER 2   If you think being silent is going to help you. If you think that.

OFFICER 1   If you think that, you don't know anything about this.

OFFICER 2   Maybe you got into this the wrong way. Maybe you think you know the way out. But you don't. The only way out is to help us.

OFFICER 1   Tell us where these individuals are. That's your play. That's your way out.

OFFICER 2   Not to freedom.

(*Officers laugh.*)

OFFICER 1   No, just out—a way to avoid the execution room.

OFFICER 2   And not just that, but even now. Even now, things can be better than they are. They don't have to be like this. There are, you can believe, better cells in the jail than the one you have. There is better food than the food you'll get. There's even, I shouldn't say this, but it could be arranged for you to go from here to a regular jail. Things are different there. Maybe better for you? There are even different guards. Things aren't all the same. You can improve your situation, that's what we're saying.

OFFICER 1   We're not your enemies. You don't have any. We're all just working together. We're all cooperating. Inspector Nagano and I are going to leave the room now. When we come back tomorrow I want you to have things to say to us. Do you understand?

Interview 1 (*Mother*)

[*Int. note.* When I visited the village, years after, I managed to conduct a series of interviews with the Oda family. It was difficult to get into contact with them, but as I have told you, I had my own reasons for trying. I had been in Japan only briefly before, and many things were new to me. I felt a beautiful feeling of opening, as though everything was expanding and sharpening, becoming larger and clearer than it had been, just as on a cloudy day, sometimes the light shifts and becomes strong when one is not even directly in sunlight. Various portions of these interviews I here include in order to show the progression of Oda Sotatsu's incarceration. I will explain it precisely, piece by piece, presenting you the evidence as I received it. The house in which I conducted the interviews was a rented house on a property known to be full of butterflies in certain seasons. At the time in which I arrived, and when I began the interviews, there were no butterflies evident. However, when we sat in the north room of the house, where Sotatsu's mother most often chose to be interviewed, she spoke of having visited the house under other circumstances, and of having seen the butterflies. For me, it was as though I had then seen them, and later, when they did indeed come, it was exactly as she had said. I say this only to give a sense of her reliability, although, clearly, a matter of insects and the matter of her son's confession are not really alike, not really. Still, the impression of exactitude remains, and so I explain it.]

[These are excerpts from long conversations, and so they may refer to things previously stated, or may begin in the midst of an idea, when something important had begun to be said.]

三

INT. Mrs. Oda, you were speaking of that first day, when you received the call from the authorities, and went to visit Sotatsu.

MRS. ODA We did not actually go that day. Neither I, nor my husband. Neither of my children.

INT. Why was that?

MRS. ODA My husband forbade it. He was horrified by the news. He sat in our house, in a room with no light on, just staring at nothing for many hours. When he came out, he said we would not go to see Sotatsu. He said he did not know anyone with that name and inquired whether I did.

INT. And what did you say?

MRS. ODA I said I did not. I did not know anyone by that name. He said he was sorry to hear about the confusion, and that the police thought we knew anyone like that, but we did not. I wanted to go, of course. Of course, I wanted to go. But, he was very clear about how it had to be.

INT. What about your other children?

MRS. ODA They were not living in our home at that time, and I hadn't contacted them.

INT. So, what changed? Why did you go to visit Sotatsu?

MRS. ODA When I woke up in the morning, my husband was wearing some clothing I hadn't seen him wear, an old suit, somewhat formal. He said it was possibly his fault, that we should see our son Sotatsu. I told him I thought that we should also. He said that didn't matter, what we should do, but that we would do it. So, we went to the car and drove to the jail.

INT. And what did you find there?

MRS. ODA The officers did not want to look at us. I don't think anyone looked us in the eye on that visit, or any other visit. They wanted to pretend we didn't exist. I understand that, by the way. I understand how it would be. Such a job, to be at a jail. It is good that someone chooses to do it, I guess.

INT. Was he far inside in the police station?

MRS. ODA They moved his cell around. He wasn't always in the same spot. Maybe because of discipline? He was often being punished, which his father agreed with. When I said I thought it was quite much that was being done, Mr. Oda told me that indeed, no, it was quite little. I don't know much about these things. If you speak to my husband, he can perhaps remember more, or remember knowing more.

INT. But the visit itself? You spoke to him?

MRS. ODA We spoke. He did not. He was in a small cell at first. There wasn't anything else in there at all, just a drain. I think they wanted him to start talking, but he wouldn't. He looked very small in the prison clothing. I didn't like to see it. I don't like to think about it now.

INT.   I'm sorry, but can you just recall what you said to him?

MRS. ODA   I don't believe I said anything. I was afraid to say the
           wrong thing and then that Mr. Oda would have it that
           we never visited again, so I stayed quiet. I wanted to
           see how he would say what it was that there was to say.
           He said, *Son, you did this? They say you did this and that you
           said so, that you said you did. Did you do this?* And Sotatsu
           said nothing. But he looked at us.

THE NARITO DISAPPEARANCES

[*Int. note.* I felt a word about the Narito Disappearances was in order at this point. Permit me to interrupt the narrative a moment for clarity's sake. It was to this crime that Oda Sotatsu confessed. When he signed the confession, it is my opinion he was somehow unaware that the crime had been carried out.]

≡

The Narito Disappearances occurred in the villages near Sakai in the year of 1977. They began around June and continued up until the capture of Oda Sotatsu. The newspapers eagerly followed the case and it drew national press attention, culminating in a furor at Oda Sotatsu's arrest. What was it?

Eight people disappeared, roughly two per month. There was no evidence of a struggle; however, it was clear that the disappearances were effected suddenly (food set out on the table, no personal objects missing, etc.). The people who disappeared were all older men and women, between the ages of fifty and seventy, who without exception lived alone. On the door of the residences a playing card was discovered, one per residence. No fingerprints of any kind were on the cards. No one witnessed the departure of any of the disappeared individuals. It was a powerful and gripping mystery, and as more and more people disappeared, the region went into shock. Patrols were even created to visit the homes of isolated or widowed individuals. But the patrols were never in the right place at the right time.

Interrogation 2

Sixteenth of October, 1977. Oda Sotatsu. Inspectors' names unrecorded.

[*Int. note.* Again, transcript of session recording, possibly altered or shoddily made. Original recording not heard.]

☰

OFFICER 1   Mr. Oda, now that you have slept, perhaps you feel differently than yesterday?

ODA   (silent)

OFFICER 2   It is impossible for you, for things to get better for you, if you do not speak at all. You have signed a confession. You do not want a lawyer or any representation. You know what you did. We are concerned with finding the individuals mentioned, those individuals mentioned in your confession.

ODA   Is it possible that I could see it? I would like to see the confession.

OFFICER 2   That is impossible. You cannot see the confession. You wrote the confession. You know what it says. This isn't a game. Tell us where to look. Where did you go with those people? Mr. Oda, our patience is growing thin.

OFFICER 1   You cannot see the confession. The inspector is correct. It is completely unnecessary. It is possible, of course, that if you cooperate, many things that are unnecessary can occur. As we said, better food, a larger cell, a different facility. Perhaps even this. I do not say yes, not at all. I don't say that. But speak to us about these things and we will see what can happen.

OFFICER 2   This is about you. This is in your hands.

(Forty more minutes of quiet on the tape as the interviewers and Oda stare at one another. Finally, the sound of a door closing, and the tape clicks off.)

Interview 2 (*Brother*)

[*Int. note.* This interview also was conducted at the house previously mentioned. Sotatsu's brother, Jiro, was his most loyal supporter. He actually learned about what had happened and tried to visit the station prior to his parents. However, he was turned away, for reasons unknown. Perhaps the first interrogation had not yet happened at the time of his visit. It is unclear. I spoke to him at great length. Of all the family, he was the one most angry about what had happened. He had worked at a steel plant as a younger man, and was doing so in 1977. He later became active in organized labor. When I met him he was well dressed and drove an expensive car. Of his personal habits, I can say he smoked nearly an entire pack of cigarettes during each one of our conversations. I don't know if this was usual for him, or if my presence and the subject of our discussions made him nervous. On several of the interviews, he was accompanied by his children, both young, who played in the yard while we spoke. Although he was very matter of fact, and even at times hostile with me, he was exceptionally soft-spoken with them. I had done judo for a while, and Jiro had also done so; at one point he broke in, out of the blue, to ask if I had ever done it. I had never said a word on the subject. When I answered yes, he laughed. I can always tell, he said. A judo man walks a bit differently. While this may have predisposed me to liking him, I assure you, I have tried at all times to be as objective as possible.]

≡

INT.   That was the nineteenth of October?

JIRO   It may have been. I don't know.

INT.   But it was your first time inside the police station?

JIRO   Actually, no, I had been there once before, in connection with a friend from the mill. I had been visiting him, accompanying his wife to visit him. I think he had been fighting and was taken by the police.

INT.   Your friend?

JIRO   Yes, that was some years before that.

INT.   But on this visit . . .

JIRO   I saw Sotatsu. The police frisked me. I signed some papers, showed some identification, and was taken in. His cell was at the back. He was there, by himself, in a long cell with no window.

INT.   Did the police leave you alone to speak with him?

JIRO   No. One of the officers stayed within earshot. When Sotatsu saw me, he came to the edge of the cell and we looked at each other.

INT.   How did he look?

JIRO   Terrible. He was in jail. How do you think he looked?

INT.   What did you say?

JIRO   I didn't say anything. I hadn't come there to say anything. I just wanted to see him and I wanted him to know that I was thinking of him. I don't know that I wanted to hear him say anything. I don't know what he could have said that would have been worth hearing.

INT.   You had read about the matter in the newspaper?

JIRO   Yes, it was all over the newspaper. It had been for months already, all about the disappearances. Then, it became all about Sotatsu. He confessed to it all, even to parts that the newspapers hadn't known anything about. That's what made the police sure. They had thought there were eight disappearances, but he had confessed to eleven, and the other three had been entirely unreported. When the police went to check on those people, they were gone too.

INT.   And you didn't ask him about it?

JIRO   I just said that. I saw him and left.

INT.   And you had other visits like that?

JIRO   I came every day. Some days they would let me in. Some days they wouldn't. When they would it was always the same. I would approach the bars from one side, he from another. Neither one of us spoke. It was said there was a room where prisoners received visitors. I never saw that room.

Interrogation 3

Nineteenth of October, 1977. Oda Sotatsu. Inspector's name unrecorded.

[*Int. note.* Again, transcript of session recording, possibly altered or shoddily made. Original recording not heard.]

☰

OFFICER 3   Mr. Oda, I have been informed about your case by the inspector you spoke to previously. He declared you unresponsive. It is his opinion that you should simply be run through the system. *Flushed out of the system.* Those were his exact words. Not to be vulgar, but you see what I mean. You are getting a particular reputation around here. I am going to explain something to you. In jail and in prison, even here at a police station, a local police station like this, there are things that people have done that make them what they are. Do you see? I was in the military, I went to school, I was in a training program, after that I joined the force, and I have worked my way up to being an inspector. That is what I am. Those things I did have made me what I am. You, on the other hand. You have done a crime. That is why you are here. What you are is a prisoner. That is what you are. However, what you are does not determine how you are treated, not the way you would think. What determines how you are treated in here is how you behave and how that behavior creates a reputation. I have a reputation for being good to the people I talk to. Then more people talk to me, then more people learn that I am good to talk to. That is my reputation. There are prisoners here who are treated exceptionally well. Some who have done worse things than others are treated better than the others. Do you know why that is?

ODA   (silent)

OFFICER 3 It is because they have learned how to behave and how to represent a particular reputation, to make it real. You are creating a reputation for yourself. Do you know that?

ODA   (silent)

OFFICER 3 There is a reason you sleep in a concrete cell with no bed, night after night. There is a reason that you get the food that no one else wants. Not all the prisoners get sprayed with a hose. Do you see what I mean? These officers are from good families. They grew up in your town. You may even know them. They have children. They treat people well. But when they see you, they think: here is an animal. Here is a person who wants nothing to do with being human, with being part of our community.

(Officer takes a deep breath, pauses.)

OFFICER 3 What we want is for you to tell us more. The information in the confession is not enough. It is very little. It is almost a useless document, other than where you are concerned. Where you are concerned, it is probably the end of you. But for others, it is useless. We need you to tell us more. Tell us more and we can help you. When I came here, today, and I was told that

I would be the one to speak to you, I had an idea about who you were. There had been talk about you. Also, the newspapers. They have been running stories. Many things about you. So, I had an idea about what you would be like. But you aren't like that. To me, you look like a regular guy, who ended up in a bad spot. You look like maybe you need to talk to someone. Like maybe all this can be explained somehow. I'm the guy you want to talk to. Think about it.

(Tape recorder clicks off.)

Interview 3 (*Mother*)

[*Int. note.* To this visit, Mrs. Oda brought a toy that had been Sotatsu's. It was a long stick painted blue with a red bell on the end. The bell was shaped like a flower. It did not make any noise, Mrs. Oda explained. It had originally been given to Sotatsu's brother as a present, and he immediately broke it. Sotatsu had found the broken toy and began carrying it around all the time. It became his. He even claimed that he could hear the sound of the bell, although clearly the bell made no sound. Once, the family played a trick on him and hid little bells in their clothing. When he would move the stick, one of the family members would surreptitiously jingle a bell. This caused him great concern and difficulty, and both parents regretted having done it; so said Mrs. Oda. It also confirmed him in his belief that there truly was a sound, and even after their ruse had been explained to him, he disbelieved it.]

Ξ

INT.   Your next visit to Sotatsu was some weeks later?

MRS. ODA   One week later. I brought him a blanket, but they wouldn't let him have it. They said he had all the blankets he needed.

INT.   He was provided with blankets by the jail?

MRS. ODA   I do not believe so. What they were saying was . . .

INT.   That he shouldn't have a blanket. Or that his sort shouldn't . . .

MRS. ODA   I think so. They did let me stand there with the blanket and try to speak with him. I told him that we were all thinking of him, and I tried something that a friend of mine said.

INT.   What do you mean by that?

MRS. ODA   A friend of mine, an older woman whose opinion I respected greatly. She said to me to do something when I went and I did. I worked it out carefully and did it. What it was was this: I should tell him a memory I had, very clearly and just speak of it, let it all move there by itself without me or the sad time we were in, just by itself, the past moment. So, I had remembered a time that would be good to speak of, that I thought I could do . . .

INT.   Did you prepare it ahead of time?

MRS. ODA   Yes, I thought about it a few ways and tried it out. Then when I went I said it to him.

INT.   Would you want to say it now the way you said it, do you think you could still remember it?

MRS. ODA   Yes. I remember. I actually said it to him several times. He seemed to like it, so when I went there I said it a few times.

INT.   And could you say it now?

MRS. ODA   I can. Let me think a minute and I will be ready.

INT.   That's fine. Do you want me to stop the tape?

MRS. ODA: Just for a minute.

[*Int. note.* Here I stopped the tape for approximately fifteen minutes while Mrs. Oda went about remembering her words. I got a glass of water for her from the kitchen and found something to do in another room. When I returned, she was ready.]

INT.   The tape-device is recording.

MRS. ODA   I said to him, I said: When you were four, your father and I had a thought that we should perhaps travel to different waterfalls, that it might be a good thing to see all the waterfalls we could. So, we began to go to waterfalls whenever we had a chance. That year I believe we saw thirty waterfalls, in many places. We developed a routine for it. We would drive there and get out. Your father would pick you up. He would say to you, *Is this the right waterfall?* and you would say, *No, not this one. Not this one.* We went all over. There are really more waterfalls than one thinks. When he talked to me about the project, I said, I don't know how many waterfalls there are to go to, but I was wrong, there are many. It was just the three of us in the car then, as your sister and brother weren't born yet. Just the three of us, riding along. We would go down these tiny roads, past fields and rice paddies. We would have to stop to ask directions of the strangest people. But everyone seemed to understand what we were doing. It was never hard to explain it. We are going to see many waterfalls. And the person would say that that was a good thing to do, and that right that way was another waterfall, a very fine one, quite worth seeing. Then we would go on down the road, and pull up at the place. I would get out, I would get you out. You would go to your father. Then the two of you, the two of you would go to the edge of the water. Your father would cock his ear to listen, and you would imitate him. We didn't have a camera, so I don't have any pictures of it. But the two of you would listen to the waterfall for quite a while. Then he would pick you up and he would say, *Son, is this the right waterfall?* and you would say, *No, not this one. Not this one.* Then we would sit and have some food that we had brought. We would look at the waterfall some more and sometimes talk about what was particular about it. Then we would get in the car and go. Your father would never look back at the waterfall as we were leaving, but you would always turn around as best you could and try to look out the window or over the backseat to see it as we drove away. When finally we had been going for months and seen many many waterfalls, we went to one that we had missed, one that was actually rather close to where we lived. It was a rainy day. It had started out pleasant, with blue skies and fine white clouds, but while we were driving there came many gray clouds that were nearly black from the north and west and with them all kinds of rain. Your father did not want to stop. It was very close, this waterfall, he said, and it was a part of the expedition that we would not turn back. So, we got there in the rain and when we did, the rain cleared. We sat in the car for a few minutes and then got out. It was a very small waterfall, one of the smaller ones we had seen. That was probably why no one said anything about it to us when we were trying to find the waterfalls. But when you and your father had listened for a while, and when he lifted you up and he asked you, *Son, is this the right waterfall?* you laughed and laughed. You didn't say anything, you just laughed and laughed. And so he said to you again, *Is this the right one? Is this it, the right waterfall?* and you said, *Yes, this is the one we have been looking for.* Then when your sister and brother were born, and we would go on family picnics, we often went there, but we did not talk about our waterfall expedition, and because you had been so young, you never remembered it. You didn't know why that was the waterfall we always went to, or that you had chosen it from all the waterfalls we had seen. We didn't know anyway, why it was the right one, your father and I. Or maybe he knows, but I don't know.

(Mrs. Oda begins to cry. I pass her a handkerchief. She refuses it.)

INT.   And did he say anything to that?

MRS. ODA   He watched me the whole time, sitting with his back to the wall, he was watching me very closely. His eyes changed while I was watching so I knew that it affected him, and that is why I came back and said it again and again. I felt that it was affecting him, whether he would talk or not.

Int. Note

The guards I spoke to said Oda dealt poorly with being in jail.

Of course, the newspapers were readily available to the guards and so they read about Oda and about what had happened, and were deeply prejudiced against him on account of the confession he had signed, which seemed to reveal his guilt beyond any doubt.

This is a peculiar matter, because the confession should not have been available to the press. Indeed, the actual confession was not. However, it seems that on the evidence of: a. witnesses seeing Oda Sotatsu dragged away from his house, and b. data from an anonymous source supplied to the press, the newspapers gained the knowledge they needed to investigate further, at which point perhaps police officials disclosed information. What happened precisely is unknown. That there were many newspaper accounts linking the Narito Disappearances to Oda Sotatsu via his own signed confession is beyond doubt.

This led to Oda being dealt with harshly, most particularly because he would not cooperate. He was kept separate from the other prisoners, and visited almost constantly by a series of officials attempting to get information from him. The interrogations that have been made available to me form a part of this narrative, as you know, but are, I suspect, the least part of the many interrogations that took place. It is clear that the guards often would not allow him to sleep ahead of an interrogation in the hopes that it would weaken his will. However that may be, it appears, from the transcripts that we have, that it was not an effective strategy in this case.

Oda Sotatsu was in jail at the police station for a period of twenty days prior to charges being brought. He was then moved to a different facility, for the trial. The entire case was evidently expedited, possibly because of the enormous media scrutiny, and as well because of the confession, and because Oda refused to deal with any potential representation he would have in court.

Interview 4 (*Sister*)

[*Int. note.* Oda Minako, Sotatsu's sister, was living elsewhere, possibly in Korea, when I began this series of interviews. It was important enough to her, when the family spoke about what I was doing, that she chose to return to Japan for some days to speak to me. These interviews also took place in the house I had let. She was an attractive woman, older, of course, and dressed very professionally. It seems she had acquired an advanced education, and was actually a professor at a university in Korea, in what subject I do not recall. She had been away at her studies when Sotatsu was apprehended by the police, and she returned from Tokyo to visit him. She was uncertain of the day, or whether her visits followed or preceded those of other family members. She did say that a childhood friendship with one of the police officers permitted her to actually enter the cell and sit with him, something allowed none of the other family members, and something mentioned by no other source.]

≡

INT.   You were there then, sitting beside him in the cell. You were a young woman, in the midst of her Ph.D., called away into what must have been as absurd a situation as you had ever dealt with.

MINAKO   I was angry with him. He had never lied, not once, and so I was sure that the confession was true. I was worried about the people who had gone missing. I knew two of them personally, an experience the rest of my family did not have, and so . . .

INT.   And so it was more complicated for you?

MINAKO   You could say so, but I expect it was more than com-
            plicated for all of us.

INT.   Of course, I don't mean to say . . .

MINAKO   I know, I understand. I just meant that my loyalties,
            my immediate duties in the situation were twofold. I
            wanted simultaneously to help my brother, a person I
            loved as much as I had ever loved anybody. I preferred
            him, in fact, preferred him to Jiro, to my mother, to my
            father. He was the only other one who actually read,
            who encouraged my studies. He wrote a great deal of
            poetry. He was cultured, although I don't know that
            anyone besides me knew that. I don't believe he shared
            that with anyone . . . I wanted to help him, but I also
            wanted to find these two people who were missing, a
            woman who had been my violin teacher, and a man,
            a Shinto priest whom I had visited as a child. I was
            deeply concerned that they should be missing, and
            I felt the guilt of their disappearance keenly. If there
            was something I could do to help them, I must do it,
            so I told myself.

INT.   And that led to you behaving in a certain way?

MINAKO   One can't say how one behaved or why, really. Such
            situations, they are far more complex than any either/
            or proposition. It is simplistic to produce events in
            pairs and lean them against each other like cards. I
            suppose if you are playing go or shogi, then such a
            thing might be helpful, but that is not life.

INT.   But you might have simply done things to make his time more bearable, irrespective of his guilt, or, alternately, tried to query him about the crime itself.

MINAKO   I did the latter. I sat by him and I told him that he was my brother, that I did not refuse him any family connection based on what happened, but that I needed to know if these people could be helped, or . . .

INT.   Or?

MINAKO   Or if they were beyond help.

INT.   And did he speak to you?

MINAKO   He did not. He watched me as I came in. He sat by me. He held my hand. When I left, we embraced. But there was no speech. It was as though he had become pre-literate. The expressiveness of his manner was magnified. His actions no longer leaned on his words. All that he meant he meant through his face and eyes, his hands.

INT.   And what did those tell you? How did they speak to you?

MINAKO   That there wasn't any hope in him, none at all. That he was waiting to die, and did feel, did indeed feel that he was not any part of any community, not ours, not any.

INT.   But he embraced you.

MINAKO   I initiated the embrace. It might have been as much out of habit as anything else. Or out of boredom. Who can say? He had been in the cell a long time.

INT.   His silence, were you prepared for it by the way he had been as a boy?

MINAKO Everything is contextual. No situation he had been in as a boy was anything like the one I found him in.

Interview 5 (*Brother*)

[*Int. note.* When Jiro discovered that Minako had come to be interviewed, he cautioned me against her. He said that she had always
been against Sotatsu, that she had enjoyed the prestige that his
crime had afforded the family (a peculiar point, and one I did not
understand), and that it was in part due to her intervention that
Sotatsu's case had gotten worse. I absorbed this information, but
did not act on it in any regard.]

≡

INT.   So you had visited him a half dozen times, simply
         sitting with him, before this visit that you just began
         speaking of?

JIRO   As I described before, I simply sat with him. I didn't
         expect I could accomplish anything else. I was a
         young man, and had no idea what I would say, or if
         there was anything to say.

INT.   But then you had this outburst.

JIRO   Yes, I had the outburst, on my eighth or ninth visit.

INT.   Can you describe the events that led to the outburst?

JIRO   Things had become bad for us in the town. No one
         would speak to my mother. Only my very best friends
         would tolerate me, and even then, only in private. My
         father, who had been a fisherman all his life, could no

longer sell his fish. No one would buy them. It came to a head one day when my father went to the store to buy something. I don't know what he was buying, but the store clerk wouldn't serve him. They got into an argument that went out into the street. Apparently the grandfather of the store clerk was one of the people who was missing. They were shouting at each other. I wasn't there, I only know what people say about what happened.

INT.   And what do they say?

JIRO   That he was denying Sotatsu's guilt. He was saying Sotatsu hadn't done it. He just kept repeating it over and over, and although the clerk had been the one who was aggressive at first, denying him service and chasing him out of the store, my father became aggressive in the street. He was just shouting at everyone, getting in people's faces—not behavior anyone had ever seen. He kept saying, *He didn't do it. He didn't do it. You know him from a boy. You know him. He didn't do it.* The crowd grew, and became angry. Someone hit him. He fell down. Other people began to hit him. He got hit and many people stepped on him before the police arrived. He was badly hurt and had to go to the hospital. And that's when it got bad.

INT.   How so?

JIRO   At the hospital, they wouldn't receive him. So, he had to be driven to a different hospital where they did take him.

INT.   How could that be, that the hospital wouldn't take him?

JIRO   I believe the presiding doctor was connected with a victim of the Disappearances also.

INT.   And so, this is all prelude to your visit, no?

JIRO   That day I went to see Sotatsu. He knew nothing of any of this, and was the same as he had always been, just sitting in the cell. When he saw me, he stood up and came to the bars. I looked at him and I thought, is there something I can see, some change in him that would make him a different person than the one I knew? I looked at him very carefully. I wanted to see who it was I was looking at. And it wasn't anyone else. It was my brother, Sotatsu. I had always known him. It was absurd that he had done these things. He hadn't done them. I was suddenly completely sure. I said to him, I said, *Brother, I know you didn't do these things. I don't know where this confession came from, but it isn't true. I know this.* And I took his hand through the bars.

INT.   The guards let you touch his hand?

JIRO   I don't remember what the officers were doing. They were watching, but they didn't stop us. I don't think they felt that Sotatsu was any danger. If you had ever seen him, you would not think him any danger.

INT.   And what did he say, you said he spoke then, what did he say?

JIRO   He said, *Brother, I didn't do anything. I didn't do it.*

INT.   And what did you say? You must have been shocked.

JIRO   I was not shocked. It was what I expected. I said to
         him that he hadn't done it, because I believed he hadn't
         done it, and then he replied, confirming what I said. It
         was all very clear.

INT.   But there must have been some relief on your part?

JIRO   I don't know about that. All of a sudden there appeared
         a huge mountain to climb where there hadn't been
         anything before. Now it was a matter of trying to get
         him out. Before that it was just visiting, just standing.
         So, my mind was racing.

INT.   And you said something to him?

JIRO   I told him he needed to get a lawyer to visit him, and he
         needed to sign a document protesting the confession,
         refusing it. I told him I would go and apply for the
         lawyer to visit, if he would agree to it. But he became
         hesitant. *I don't know,* he said. *I don't think it matters.* So,
         I tried to convince him that it mattered, I don't know
         what I said, but when I left, he had agreed to speak to
         the lawyer and tell the lawyer what he told me. I left,
         and went straight to visit my father in the hospital.
         My mother was there, and I told them. My mother
         was just shaking. She didn't cry, just sat there shaking.
         My father had many bandages and such. He seemed
         to stiffen. He said, *Why did he sign the confession, ask him
         that.* I said that I hadn't thought to ask him that. He
         said I should have thought of that. I apologized for not

having thought of that. He was always very hard on me, my father.

INT.   And then you went to make the application for the lawyer's visit?

JIRO   I did.

INT.   And the lawyer was scheduled to visit after three days, you said.

JIRO   Then I went to see my brother again. That was the next day, I think. I had to work, so I visited him late. He seemed happy to see me, for the first time. I asked him why he had signed the confession. If he hadn't done it, why had he signed it? He said he couldn't speak about it. I said he would have to. He became quiet again. I couldn't get any more out of him. So, I stood there for about forty-five minutes hoping he would change his mind and speak. He didn't. I reminded him I was coming with the lawyer and I left.

INT.   What day was this?

JIRO   I don't know what day. This was so long ago! He had been in jail for at least two weeks by this time. I got up the next day and went to see my father, before going on shift at the factory. I was still feeling hopeful. I thought maybe the lawyer could convince him to talk about it. When I got to the hospital, my father was much improved. They were going to release him that day. He could walk around on his own. I told him the news, that I had gotten the lawyer to come, and that I

had tried to find out about the confession. He was very
cold.

INT.   What did he say?

JIRO   He has always been cold to me. I don't think he ever
liked me. But this time he was very hard. What had
happened to him, maybe it used up something that he
had. Now he had no more of it. He told me that I was
a fool. That I was running errands for a fool and that
I was a fool. My sister came in while he was talking. I
hadn't even known she was there. I thought she was in
Tokyo. They both started talking about how Sotatsu
had signed the confession and it must be true. How I
was always believing people, that I was foolish, that I
should let people with better judgment take charge of
things. They said it was clear he had done the crime,
the thing now was to get him to admit it in a way that
would save him being executed. This other thing, of
him being innocent, was just a fantasy, a fantasy I had
put on him. When I described how I had told Sotatsu
that I thought he was innocent, and that my words
had made him speak to me about being innocent, my
sister became angry. She told me that I was stupid,
going around behaving this way, that I should not put
a stick into a beehive. My father agreed. He told me to
go away, that he would see me once he was at home,
but that he just wanted to rest now. He was going
to go home later that day, but for now, he wanted to
rest. I left with my sister, and she told me again that
I was an idiot for causing my father more harm and
worry when he had already been put in the hospital,
been beaten up, had nearly died. I apologized. I was

confused and, again, I keep saying this, but I was very young and didn't know very much. Now, I would act differently, I think, but then, my sister had always been the one who was right. My father also. I had been a disappointment to both of them.

(End of tape.)

Interview 6 (*Brother*)

[*Int. note.* The brother left the day before without concluding our interview. He had evidently found it difficult speaking of the relations among himself, his father, and his sister. I think it points to how important Sotatsu was to him that he would even consider disclosing these things to me, a stranger. He had an enormous desire, Jiro, to get the complete and true account of these things across. I had come to believe he disliked me; in fact, I'm almost sure of it. However, he also believed that I was going to do the thing properly. In his work with unions, he perhaps had gotten used to compromises, to making compromises and working with people he disliked. Nonetheless, it was difficult for him to speak in this manner, so we stopped for the day and the next day we resumed.]

☰

INT.   So, you went from the hospital, from seeing your sister, directly to the jail?

JIRO   I could not; I had to work. I went to the police station when my shift was done, perhaps at eight in the evening. When I got there, I saw a person leaving, a girl I knew Sotatsu had been familiar with.

INT.   She had been his girlfriend?

JIRO   I don't believe so. I think she knew him, though. So, I assumed she had been there to see him, although it puzzled me. I thought only family were allowed visits. Evidently, she had been admitted, and admitted many times. One of the guards told me she had been coming every day. Jito Joo was her name.

INT.   Did she greet you as she passed?

JIRO   She ignored me, which was not surprising. We were not on friendly terms, and everyone in the town was ignoring me at that time.

INT.   So, what happened when you reached his cell?

JIRO   The lawyer was there already, in the station. He accompanied me to the cell. Sotatsu stood there with his back to us and he told the lawyer to leave. The lawyer was quite angry. He was very busy. Did I know he had literally hundreds of cases? Did I know he had no time for such things? I apologized as much as I could, and went with the lawyer out of the station, apologizing the whole way to the car, where the lawyer got in and drove away. When I went back into the station and the officers took me again to Sotatsu he would not speak to me. He wouldn't turn around. He stood in the middle of the cell, facing away from me. I was sure that meant he was innocent. But, if he wouldn't say it, I didn't know what to do. I went home and my girlfriend, she was waiting for me in the driveway. She told me she had taken her things. She was moving back to her parents' house. She couldn't see me anymore.

INT.   It was a bad time.

JIRO   You could say that.

INT.   And then you saw your mother at home?

JIRO   I went to their house and my father was asleep. My
        mother was washing something, a shirt or something.
        She was washing it and washing it. It didn't need to be
        washed anymore. I stood there and talked to her and
        she said that my father had made the decision and that
        was that. What was the decision, I asked. She said we
        were no longer going to talk about any Sotatsu. That
        I was now the first son, that there was no Sotatsu and
        hadn't ever been. She said my sister had gone back to
        Tokyo, my one sibling had gone back to Tokyo, and
        that we were four, that there were four of us in the
        family. I didn't say anything to this. I just left.

Interrogation 4

Second of November, 1977. Oda Sotatsu. Inspectors' names unrecorded.

[*Int. note.* Again, transcript of session recording, possibly altered or shoddily made. Original recording not heard. Furthermore, it appears that many interrogations are missing from the record, as it is absurd to conclude Sotatsu was not interrogated at all between the nineteenth of October and the second of November. This transcript is large. The inspector speaks at length on various matters, possibly trying to elicit a response from Sotatsu. He refers to previous conversations they have had, which are unrecorded. This is further evidence for the suppression of interrogation transcripts. I will note that it was not necessary at the time for these transcripts to be released, so the destruction of empty-interrogation sessions is potentially legitimate.]

≡

OFFICER 3   I want you to tell me about these cards. These are the cards you left on the doors. Why did you do that?

ODA   (silent)

OFFICER 3   Nothing in your history suggests you care at all about France, that you have any acquaintance with France. Yes, musically, we can see you have some recordings. But, beyond that, cards . . . It's unclear where you even obtained them. Tell me at least that. Where did you buy these cards?

ODA   (silent)

OFFICER 3   I am just thinking, I have a daughter who likes these sorts of things. She is kind of empty-headed, a dreamer. You know the type. She is too pretty for her own good. A father should not say such things, I know. But I think she would be better off a bit plainer but with good sense. Anyway, she would love to have cards like these. But I don't know where to get them. Where should I go to get these cards? Perhaps in Tokyo? You have a sister in Tokyo, no? Does she like cards? She studies languages, no? She speaks German, Korean, English. Does she speak French, your sister?

ODA   (silent)

OFFICER 3   Maybe I will call this sister of yours. Maybe I will send someone to ask her, does she speak French. Or you could spare me the trouble. You could just tell me. I would trust your answer.

(Tape-device clicks off.)

54

Interview 7 (*Mother*)

[*Int. note.* When I brought up the details that Jiro had spoken of, the narrative of the father's beating, Sotatsu's possible recanting of the confession, the visit of the sister, etc., Mrs. Oda became very agitated. She said that Jiro meant no good for anyone, that he was against the rest of the family and always had been. She said that he was jealous of his sister's good fortune, and that he had no sense of family responsibility. I was not to trust anything he might say. I asked her if she could speak of particular things he brought up, because I wanted to clear up the record. I wanted to make the record as clear as possible. Would she mind that?]

[She said she would not.]

≡

INT.   The first question is, what happened at the store?

MRS. ODA   You mean, when my husband had his accident?

INT.   Yes, the accident. How did that come about?

MRS. ODA   Everyone in the town had turned against us. They felt that we were just as guilty as Sotatsu. Maybe it was true, maybe it would have been true, that we were all equally guilty. That is what my husband believed. He thought it was his fault, in particular. All of a sudden, we were despised. We were the lowest ones of all. No one would speak to me. People I had spoken to for years, I would pass them in the street and they would do this thing, this stepping away. They would walk a little farther away than usual. Maybe someone else couldn't see it, but I could see it. It was very evident, this distance. Also, some would even, they would even spit on us. Children.

INT.   Children would spit on you?

MRS. ODA It happened once. From a window, a child spat on me. Mr. Oda knocked on the door of the house, but no one answered.

INT.   But we were talking about the accident.

MRS. ODA My husband went to buy some rice flour. We were out of rice flour and he wanted to buy some for me so I could do the cooking. At the store, the clerk, a mean little person, I had never liked him, never. He refused to sell my husband the flour. My husband put the money on the counter and took the rice flour. The clerk followed after my husband, saying his money was no good. He threw the money at my husband. I think he never liked my husband. He threw it on him, the money, and he shouted that he could never come in the store again. My husband tried to talk to him. He said, *You know he didn't do it. Sotatsu does not do things like that. It is a mistake.* But the man wouldn't hear of it. He just started hitting my husband with a stick, a cane of some kind. He started that, and then he was chasing him. My husband tried to run away, but others caught him and they held him down and hit him until the police came. The police didn't even check to see who had done it. They told everyone to go. The police felt it was all right for this to have been done.

INT.   And then the hospital wouldn't accept him?

MRS. ODA   The hospital wouldn't accept him. He was bleeding all over. He wasn't even awake. He was going in and out. The doctor looked at him, opened the back of the ambulance, looked at him and said that he would not receive him at that hospital, that everyone should know he would not do such a thing for the Oda family. I don't know. I ask you, how can such a person be a doctor? My husband was taken to another place where there were real doctors, an actual hospital, not like this first one. There he was taken care of. In all the years since, I have never gone to that hospital, not once. I tell my friends, also, do not go there. That is not a good place.

INT.   But the main thing I wanted to ask you about was Sotatsu telling Jiro that he hadn't done it.

MRS. ODA   We did not believe Jiro. He was always a difficult child, did poorly in school, was always lying. He was a lying child, every time he would say something it was likely to be something a person couldn't believe. You had to look at everything from three sides and even then it would turn out to be false. So, he gets it in his head he would convince Sotatsu of something. We did not believe him. Also, he picked the worst time to tell anyone about this. In the hospital room when my husband was nearly dying? He did not die, no. But he was almost dying, very close to it. My daughter came from Tokyo, just to see my husband, just because of his injuries. She did not visit Sotatsu. She was there,

and she didn't like it either, what Jiro was doing. We
were not alone.

INT.   But he is your son.

MRS. ODA   Yes, he is. He has done better for himself. Now he has
a good family. He is no longer the same. But when he
remembers that time, I do not think he can be trusted.

Interview 8 (*Mother*)

[*Int. note.* Mrs. Oda returned specifically to explain her last point. I was woken up by knocking at the door of the house where I was staying. I went downstairs and there she was. She apologized for the sudden visit, but felt there was something that must be cleared up.]

≡

MRS. ODA   I will tell you a story about Jiro. I will explain why he cannot be trusted, not really at all. He used to have a game where he would pretend that he was a lord and he would have his toys come before him and present him with cases to decide. He thought this was a very amusing game. I do not remember him ever playing it with anyone else, just alone. He would do different voices for the different toys. They did not need to be figures in order to bring a petition. His favorite spoon, for instance, was often coming. First in line, second in line, third in line—they would all argue and jostle, trying to be the first to speak to Jiro, and he would sit on a little stage he had made and argue with them or tell them what was what. Well, it would be like this: Jiro would say, who is this and what have they to say? And the little wooden box would be there in front of the spoon which was in front of the cloth bird and they would all be shouting and saying things and Jiro would hold up his hand for silence. Then there would be some quiet and he would say they would all be taken and killed if they couldn't speak in turn. Then the box would say, I don't know what it would say exactly, this was something that went on all the time, hundreds of times. Possibly the box had something it was always asking for, and never getting, I don't know. But it might say, I don't like the spot where I am put at night. Often other ones get placed on my head and it's uncomfortable, and Jiro would say, don't open your mouth again or I will have you killed, and he would send the box away. Then it was the spoon's turn. He would say that, would say the same thing every time. No matter what was said to him, he would say that, don't open your mouth again or I will have you killed. I doubt he even remembers it. This was long ago, even before he went to school.

INT.   But why do you say that he can't be trusted? I'm sorry, I don't see . . .

MRS. ODA   That he thinks everyone should receive the same treatment, regardless of what they did or what they say? Or that it doesn't matter what anyone does—it all ends up the same? Maybe he has changed some things about himself, but a boy is a boy. He is still the same one he was. Don't tell him that I told you this. Or do. I guess I don't know.

(She roots around in her bag and brings out an old soup spoon.)

MRS. ODA   This is it, I thought I would bring it to show you. For some reason, he would always have this spoon go on and on. It was like the spoon was trying the most to convince him. But it never did. I would be sitting in the next room and listening as he would play this game. I would listen to the whole game. Every time I listened, from beginning to end. The things he would have them say, you couldn't believe. But this spoon was always the one with the most elaborate excuses, the most long-winded little speeches. Always it was the same, though. Don't open your mouth again, or I will have you killed. I really pitied the spoon, so, so I still have it.

INT.   It is a keepsake, from Jiro's childhood. That's a good thing to have, and a good reason to have it.

MRS. ODA   Oh no, I don't think of it that way. I rescued it from him. I don't think he cared about the spoon at all.

Interview 9 (*Father*)

[*Int. note.* I had attempted to speak with the father on many occasions. He would agree over the telephone to meet, and then the day would come and he would simply not arrive. His wife gave many excuses: his declining health; the difficulty of travel; the day was hot, etc. When we spoke again on the telephone he would act confused. He had not known we were to meet, etc. After perhaps nine or ten such assignations, he finally arrived. He was extremely thin and small, hardly the dominating force that he had seemed to be from his family's accounts of him. However, when he spoke, there was a certain forcefulness there. Like his son, he appeared to distrust and dislike me. He felt that I was attempting to trick Mrs. Oda into telling me things that I shouldn't hear. He had come to set things straight. I was not to listen to the things that Mrs. Oda said. He wanted to make that clear. He was going to tell me some things, and that would be that. The things he would tell me would take the place of what Mrs. Oda had said, and certainly should take the place of whatever nonsense his son was feeding me. He was surprised to hear that Minako had spoken to me. He did not know she was in the country, and seemed confused by the news. It took a little while to get him back on track. He preferred to speak in the yard, so occasionally on the tape there is the sound of traffic in the distance. He said that when one was his age, any day with a fine afternoon sun like that had to be used. One had to use things when one had them, so he said.]

≡

INT.   Where shall we begin?

MR. ODA   I was not surprised when I heard the news, when I was told by our neighbor that someone had seen my son taken away to the police station. I can tell you that, Mr. Ball. I was not surprised at all. If these things took others by surprise, well, they did not take me by surprise.

INT.   Why were you not surprised? How could you possibly have guessed that such a thing would happen?

MR. ODA   I have always known that something terrible was going to come. Until then our life had gone well. I was living in the shadow of this thing, this terrible thing that no one else could see. But, I knew that it was coming. Fishermen are not like other people. We can tell things; not like priests. I am not saying we are special or deserve any regard. We deserve no regard. In fact, one might say we are the lowest ones, drudging around in the water for a lifestyle that keeps one's family poor, that never amounts to anything. But we do see things. Sometimes we see them before they happen. It is not reliable. It isn't the same as knowing about things. One doesn't find it useful, you see? Do you, do you see? It isn't a useful thing. It is just a thing. I knew something grave was coming, and when it came, I recognized it. I had seen it before, you see. It was like an old friend. Or an old enemy. One saw, though, immediately, that there were no preparations that could have been made. That sort of thing is just foolishness.

INT.   So, you thought Sotatsu was doomed? That he never would have amounted to anything?

MR. ODA   He and my brother got along very well. My brother's business was nearly ruined by that, by Sotatsu's presence. But they got on well.

INT.   Why did you not visit your son in the jail?

MR. ODA   What do you mean? I went there. I went there first, before anyone.

INT.   I'm sorry, I know that, I meant to say, why did you not visit him after that first visit? Why did you stop going?

MR. ODA   This is not the reason I came here to talk to you.

INT.   Do you have something else you want to talk about?

MR. ODA   I do. I do.

INT.   Well, tell me what you want to tell me. I am ready to hear anything you have to say.

MR. ODA   Mr. Ball, my son was ill. He was ill his whole life. He was sick once as an infant. My wife denies it, but she is a moron. He cried once for two weeks straight and his head turned blue. He recovered, but he was never the same. He was always ill with this, whatever it was. He thought he could hear bells ringing all the time. It was part of his illness. That's why he was always playing records. He wanted it out of his head.

INT.   No one else says anything about this.

MR. ODA   You shouldn't listen to the others. This is what we are saying, that I am telling you the things now that you can use. We are talking about that.

INT.   I understand that. You said that already.

MR. ODA   Maybe others couldn't see it, but I always could. I could always tell when he was about to do something stupid. He would get this blue look, this look that I recalled from his childhood. It would be like he was being strangled, but he wasn't, and you would know, you would just know—he is going to do something now that everyone will regret. And then he would do it. Of course, he would never apologize either, afterward. He would do something like, for instance, he would forget to greet me when I came in. I would just stare at him and stare at him, waiting, and the longer I stared the more I could see it building up. Then, instead of saying anything, anything at all, he'd just up and run off out of the house. And Jiro would run off too. Anything he did, Jiro would do. Only Jiro didn't have the sense that Oda sometimes had. Although now, it's not easy to say which one turned out worse.

INT.   Are you angry at Jiro for something that he has done?

MR. ODA   You come here and it is like you are going to fix something, but either the thing that is broken is part of something that is gone, or you are doing no good with the thing that is still around. I don't know why I came to talk to you.

INT.   Please, just let me ask you a few questions. You said at one point, after the accident, when you were in the hospital, you said . . .

MR. ODA   That is an invention of my wife's. I was not in the hospital. I don't know about that. She talks about it sometimes. I don't know where she got that.

INT.   All right. Well. It is said that you forbade the family from visiting with or talking about Sotatsu. That you were very angry with Sotatsu and no longer wanted to have him be a part of your family, that you specifically told your daughter, your wife, and your son not to speak to him or visit him. Is that true?

MR. ODA: I do not think that you, I think, I . . .

[*Int. note.* Here, Mr. Oda got up and left the house in great confusion, stopping occasionally to tell me that I should not speak to his wife, his son, or his daughter, that his son was not to be believed, and that he did not understand why I had come in the first place. I apologized to him for making any difficulty, and told him that I was going to use his testimony as well as any other testimony I could find because I wanted the account to be complete. He said that this was an idea with no merit, that there wasn't anything complete, that I should just leave.]

TRIAL

Int. Note: Regarding the Newspaper Coverage of the Trial

For the next section, I will provide you with the serialized coverage of the Oda Trial that ran in many newspapers throughout Japan during that time. The writer, Ko Eiji, was a well-known journalist with a particular stylistic approach that endeared him to his audience. Nonetheless, during these proceedings he provided a mostly clear delineation of opinion and fact. I will not give all of his serialization, but enough to make events apparent. His serialization can be divided into:

1. sketches of the main individuals involved
   a. Oda Sotatsu
   b. Judge X
   c. Judge Y
   d. Judge Z
   e. Prosecutor W
   f. Defense Counsel R
2. descriptions of the emotional climate in which the trial took place
3. daily account
   a. events in court
   b. notable events in jail
   c. sentencing, exit of Oda Sotatsu

That Ko was biased against Oda Sotatsu is very evident. I ask you to understand that it is almost inconceivable that he should write in a markedly unbiased manner at this time, even if he felt differently. I do not believe that he did feel differently. I believe that he wrote as he felt. However, it is simply a fact that temperatures in the Sakai region were running very high. I like to think that if I had written a contemporaneous account, I might have kept my equanimity and been a bit more forgiving than he proved to be. It is likely that such a hope is just a pretension. One may often (after the fact) criticize the play-by-play in a boxing match, but the simple fact is, the commentator must continue speaking, whatever he sees, however much or how little, however bad his position relative to the fighters.

I should note also that Ko is a pen name. It indicates a principle in Go, whereby a person must move a stone elsewhere on the board before playing back into a particular contested area. In this way, he sets himself up as a lover of complexities. You may decide for yourself if he deserves the name he has given himself.

Incidentally, this account was used by newspapers not only in Osaka Prefecture but throughout Japan.

ODA TRIAL COVERAGE [Ko Eiji]

Sketch of ODA SOTATSU.

ODA SOTATSU

Son of a fisherman, Oda Sotatsu. Twenty-nine years old. A product of the Osaka Prefecture school system. What was his work? A clerk in a thread concern. It has been several weeks since he was removed from the population, and why? He is accused of the abduction and perhaps murder of eleven of your fellow citizens. This young man, this quiet individual—it is rumored he has even confessed to the crimes. I give you now a pen sketch of Oda as he sits in the courtroom under the hard eyes of his three judges.

Hair cut rather short—perhaps expressly for the trial. It was rumored it was long when he was brought in. He sits uneasily in his chair wearing a very cheap suit, a suit, as someone once said, made to be hanged in. He is small of stature, and his gaunt cheeks express at least some of the savageness that must lurk beneath his unthreatening exterior. Most of all, most chilling of all to the observer is the despicable coldness of the eyes. Nothing anyone says seems to move him. He is in a globe of cold that refuses all human contact. We shall see if he can maintain the same air when the judges pronounce their sentence at the trial's conclusion.

ODA TRIAL COVERAGE [Ko Eiji]

Sketch of JUDGES: Judge Iguchi; Judge Handa; Judge Shibo.

JUDGE IGUCHI
The first to enter. Strength of character is evident in the line of the jaw, the poise of the shoulders. One can see that the first thing Iguchi does is to fix Mr. Oda in his gaze and to hold him there, as though a hawk has beheld a mouse. His many years of distinguished trial service recommend him to us.

JUDGE HANDA
A relative newcomer, Judge Handa has seen his share of difficult and complicated cases, and has rendered many powerful and just decisions. Known for his conduct in the Misaki trial of 1975, he was feted in the newspapers at the time. Since then he has only continued his good work. If Mr. Oda believes that Judge Handa's relative youth will be a factor in his favor, one would be startled by the optimism.

JUDGE SHIBO
It is not necessary to describe this man to the public of the Sakai region. His omnipresence in community affairs and his generosity make him a distinguished role model both for our youth and for those of us who still can change for the better. He is active as a professor in university as well as in his judicial vocation, and it is clear that the case benefits from his presence. A tall man, he is known for a habit of holding one elbow with the fingers of his opposite hand while considering a case (as shown in last year's famous and excellent judicial illustration by the artist Haruna).

I hardly think the public could be better served in this case.

ODA TRIAL COVERAGE [Ko Eiji]

Sketch of Prosecution and Defense: Prosecutor Saito, and Defense Counsel Uchiyama.

PROSECUTOR SAITO

Known for a time as the man with the 100 percent conviction rate, a prosecutor consulted for many years by other lawyers in districts far afield for his definitive opinions, Prosecutor Saito comes with the very highest possible honors to this trial. It is rumored that his pretrial investigations have led him to another certain conviction. We shall see the effect of that ourselves. It was said at one time that as a young man, Saito resembled a heron. Whether this was meant with a view to humor or to the establishment of dignity, who can say? If he remains a heron, it is one in flight. When he lands to wade in criminal waters it is a sacrifice he makes on our collective behalf.

DEFENSE COUNSEL UCHIYAMA

In fifteen years of service, the stolid Uchiyama has kept his search for the truth at the forefront of his pursuit of excellence. His sturdy build and strong face should reassure the public; he does nothing without thought for the victims, for the populace, for justice, and for the eventual absolution of the criminal. Well-known among his comrades, he has earned a fine reputation. We look forward to seeing his work in this trial.

ODA TRIAL COVERAGE [Ko Eiji]

DAY ONE

Oda Sotatsu is brought into the room. He is seated. He, Prosecutor Saito, and Defense Counsel Uchiyama await the entrance of the judges. One by one the judges enter the room and are seated.

The rumor is that while in police custody, Mr. Oda refused to speak. It is said by some in the radical press that he was treated badly, and that view may well be borne out by the poor health he appears to exhibit. However, opponents of that view would be quick to point out that remorse could easily be destroying his health. Whatever the case is, we shall see if he continues his silence into the trial.

The prosecutor and defense counsel approach the judges. Some discussion is evident. They return to their places. The prosecution presents its indictment. Oda Sotatsu is accused of the abduction and murder of eleven individuals. When the charges are read, Mr. Oda is unmoved. His knuckles are not white, his pupils do not dilate, his brow does not quiver. He is quite unmoved.

Nothing seems to touch him as Prosecutor Saito speaks, not even the reading aloud of a damning document signed by Mr. Oda himself prior to reaching police custody. It is a confession, but it is not a confession signed and countersigned legally in the eyes of the law. It may show his guilt, but whether it can be considered the equal of a properly-arrived-at-confession is a matter to be discovered in time.

The judges confer. The question is brought to Oda Sotatsu and to Defense Counsel Uchiyama:

Will Oda Sotatsu admit or deny the facts as set down in the indictment?

Oda Sotatsu speaks. It is as though he is summoning up words from deep within him, with great difficulty. At first what he says cannot be made out. Judge Shibo asks that he speak louder. He is made to speak louder. He says, *He does not know about the facts of the indictment, yet he holds to the confession that he signed, as he signed it.*

This is not good enough for the judges. Again, he is asked, concerning the facts of the indictment prepared by Prosecutor Saito, does he admit or deny them? Mr. Oda repeats himself. He does not know about the facts of the indictment, yet he holds to the confession that he signed, as he signed it. Mr. Oda is told that he has just heard the indictment. He cannot be thought ignorant of the indictment. What is being asked of him is that he simply admit or deny those facts. Mr. Oda speaks again, he says that he, while aware of the indictment, nonetheless can neither admit nor deny it, rather, he respectfully holds to the confession that he has signed, as he signed it.

Through all this, Defense Counsel Uchiyama appears greatly chagrined, but attempts to appear unmoved. Can it be he did not know this was going to happen?

The judges call for a recess. The trial will continue on the following day.

ODA TRIAL COVERAGE [Ko Eiji]

DAY TWO

Oda Sotatsu is brought into the room. He is seated. He, Prosecutor Saito, and Defense Counsel Uchiyama await the entrance of the judges. One by one the judges enter the room and are seated.

The judges announce: it has been decided that, as the general effect of the language present in the confession is a mirror to that of the indictment, it is legitimate and appropriate that admitting the facts of the confession is identical to admitting the facts of the indictment, and that as a practical matter, it shall be considered as such in this case.

The court will therefore be recessed for the day, and on the following day Prosecutor Saito will present his case.

ODA TRIAL COVERAGE [Ko Eiji]

CONDITION OF MR. ODA

It has become known that Oda Sotatsu has, at some point in the week previous, stopped eating altogether. At the point of the trial's inception, he was on the fourth or fifth day of his fast. In the radical papers, it is being called a hunger strike. We see no grounds for that, as it is not apparent that Mr. Oda's fast has any purpose, or any possible object. Certainly, Mr. Oda has not made that object known.

ODA TRIAL COVERAGE [Ko Eiji]

ATMOSPHERE IN THE PREFECTURE

While staying in the region for the trial, I have witnessed a huge outpouring of emotion. There is great hope that the trial may move Mr. Oda to confess the location of the victims of the Narito Disappearances. Whether that will happen or not is, however, completely unknown. It is even espoused in some legal circles that the trial may be lengthened in the hopes that the particular sort of pressure it exerts might be helpful in eliciting a full disclosure by Mr. Oda. Whether that will be the case or not is unclear. Certainly it appears that no effort has been spared in the selection of the individuals involved in the trial. Also, the results of Prosecutor Saito's pretrial investigation have not yet been made known. It is quite conceivable that he has discovered information that may be of use.

Ko

Interview

[*Int. note.* I had intended to give you more of Ko Eiji's serialization, but I find that I want, again and again, to intercede and explain things. Therefore, I believe, we will continue, as if on foot, together. I decided to try to find Mr. Ko; indeed, I managed to find Mr. Ko, and he consented to speak to me about the trial. I present the results of that interview below.]

[This interview took place in Ko Eiji's own home, a shabby building on the south side of Sakai. His daughter let me in, but left immediately after seeing that I was situated and given various measures of hospitality. We sat by a long series of windows looking out toward the harbor. The old journalist explained that he liked to sit there in the mornings, but that the noise became too much in the afternoon, and he would retire then to the far side of the house. I told him that the interview would likely not take such a long time as that.]

≡

INT.   Mr. Ko, I wonder if you would give an explanation of the final days of the trial of Oda Sotatsu. Your coverage of it was quite sensational at the time, and syndicated throughout the country. How did events play out?

KO   He simply wouldn't speak. There were, I suppose, many things he might have said. He said none of them. Apart from the moment when he was made to speak, at the trial's beginning, he did not speak again. It simply wasn't the way a prisoner should behave, certainly not the way an innocent man would. The whole thing defied reason. If it was a joke, it was the strangest joke in the world, and for a person to risk his own life, and with no sense of what anything might mean? I just don't know.

INT.   Some have said that the forced feeding that went on, that may have made him willful. Do you believe that view?

KO   Certainly, after the fourth day of trial when he was becoming seriously ill from his fast, that's when they began to feed him. I think then there was a definite change in his manner. While his behavior was outwardly the same, he seemed resigned. There was even less to be found in his eyes than before.

INT.   And you were all hoping that he would speak about the victims?

KO   The judges questioned him repeatedly and at great length about the victims. It was to no avail. His own lawyer, I believe it was Yano Haruo, the defense counsel...

INT.   It was Mr. Uchiyama, I believe.

KO   Oh, yes, dear me, it has been so many years. Uchiyama Isao. He is dead, I believe. Just a few years back. A man with a large family. They have always lived in Sakai, I believe, many generations.

INT.   You were saying that the defense counsel...

KO   The defense counsel, let me see ... ah, yes, the defense counsel even tried to convince him, tell all, please tell all, it will be the best for you and all concerned. He really was a good man, a very good, just man, Uchiyama. Very respected. He tried everything he could with Oda. I spoke to him alone about it, long afterward. It was a great regret of his, the whole thing. Some blamed him. Unfairly, but, well, some did. Uchiyama told me he kept a picture of Oda in his house for many years, the rest of the time he was practicing, just to remind him—we know so little about our fellow men. There is always more to know. Do you know what he said to me? What Uchiyama said? On the day he retired, he tore the picture up and threw it out. He didn't want to look at it anymore. I think he felt he had tried with Oda. He had begged him to speak and explain himself. But Oda was unmoved.

INT.   And the result was?

KO   The result was that the trial came to an end. He wouldn't speak, and the facts seemed relatively clear. He had said in his confession that the twelve victims were taken from this place and that place, all information that was nowhere else to be found, not in the newspapers, nowhere. I think the newspapers had only known about some of the victims anyway. There is a burden, a revelation of secret that has to occur— and that was it. The confession is never enough on its own, or shouldn't be. Perhaps it sometimes is. It shouldn't be. In this case there was more. All these people had disappeared. You have to understand, we were very concerned. Everyone in Sakai, in Osaka Prefecture, we were very concerned.

INT.   I do, I appreciate that.

KO There was just no way anyone could have known.

INT. And the sentence—did Mr. Oda accept it in the same spirit that he accepted the rest?

KO The sentence was, as you know, he would be hanged. He would go to a prison and wait for some time, and thereafter be hanged. Some had spoken of leniency in the case, based on his silence, his aberrant behavior. Perhaps he was mad? He did not appear mad to me, or to the judges. No one in the room thought he was mad. The work of the court is to give justice, it is the one measure of a society, when all other measures are abandoned. How do you give justice? Here we had twelve . . .

INT. Eleven, I believe.

KO Yes, yes, eleven victims. Who was to speak for them?

INT. But the reading of the sentence. Did it affect him?

KO Not noticeably. I believe he was aware that it would come. It was not a surprise to any of us.

INT. I will read to you what you wrote on that occasion. You wrote, *So ends the long, painful story of the Narito Disappearances. Sadly, we know as little at the end as we did at the beginning. We have found someone to blame for it, but are no better equipped to factually answer the question, where are our lost family members and why were they taken? These are secrets it seems that Oda Sotatsu will bear with him to the grave. May they give him no solace there.*

(A minute's pause.)

INT.   How does that sound to you now?

(Tape-device clicks off.)

[*Int. note.* Here Ko Eiji chose to stop the interview.]

Int. Note

[That afternoon, I left Ko Eiji's house and went to the industrial area round about. I walked for a very long time, eventually making my way back to the hotel where I was staying. When I got there, his daughter was sitting outside on a bench. She said there was something more her father wanted to tell me. Would I come back with her right then? I agreed, and we hailed a cab. It was pleasant, riding in a cab with this young woman who so clearly disapproved of me and of my treatment of her father. She did not like having been dispatched on such an errand. When we got to the house, she unlocked the door, and we went up the stairs. She showed me to where her father was, and again went away. I don't actually know if this was even Ko Eiji's daughter. Perhaps it was his assistant or amanuensis. I certainly didn't ask. Yet one would imagine, if she had been his helper, she would not have been so reluctant to go here and there on his errands. Who can say? I sat down and turned on my tape-device.]

≡

KO   Let's not worry about that for a moment.

(He brings out a shogi board.)

KO   Do you play?

INT.   Badly. I am much better at . . .

KO   at Western chess, I suppose?

(Laughs.)

INT.   Yes, certainly.

KO   Do you know how the pieces move?

INT.   I do. I believe I do. You might have to remind me of a rule or two.

KO   Then let us play a game.

[We played three games of shogi, and in each I was soundly beaten. When the games were over, we sat for a while, not saying anything. Ko Eiji's assistant brought us something hot to drink. The light changed slowly as the streetlamps lit up all along the roads and avenues. The day lasted longest out on the water, but even there it eventually fell away, perhaps most completely.]

KO   I don't like the way this ended, our conversation. That's why I asked you back.

INT.   Our conversation?

KO   Our conversation. I don't like this conclusion. I have something else to say. This is what it is: I went there to the prison during the fast.

INT.   To see Sotatsu?

KO   To see him.

INT.   And what did you see?

KO   He was weak and tired, but the guards woke him up. The chief guard on duty accompanied me and they made a big show of presenting Oda with his food, which he did not eat. It was strange, and at the time, I felt odd about it. Now I feel, well, you see, it isn't clear, not even now, which way it was.

INT.   Whether . . .

KO   Whether they were starving him or not. But they put this food in front of him and he didn't eat it. I saw that. My photographer took pictures of him and we left. I looked him in the eye, or tried to. But, I saw nothing. He didn't appear to even see me. I suppose I looked like any of the others.

INT.   But you weren't like the others?

KO   I was a journalist. I was trying to see what was there.

INT.   But even with that, you . . .

KO   Yes, even then, I failed.

INT.   Can you say . . .

KO   I want you to know it wasn't that easy for me—not as easy as the newspaper accounts make it sound. We knew so little. I just, I couldn't understand it. Well . . .

(Silence on the tape for another minute, and then it clicks off.)

Room Like a Gallows Tree

Int. Note: Transfer to Death Row

Following the trial, Oda Sotatsu was transferred from the jail where he was being held to an actual prison. Within that prison, he was placed on what is known as death row. Oda Sotatsu did not appeal the verdict of his trial, or the sentence of death by hanging. He merely continued in silence. His family did not visit him at the prison, with the exception of his brother, Jiro, who came as often as he could. There was one other visitor: Jito Joo. But that account will follow in the second section of this book. For now, we shall proceed through the last months of Oda Sotatsu. The information we have about this time comes from Jiro, and from interviews I have conducted with men who were guards.

Interview 10 (*Brother*)

[*Int. note.* In the meantime, Jiro had heard about my interview with his father, and had heard of the argument that had broken out (in his father's estimation). It seems that by turning his father against me, I had obtained some measure of trust from Jiro. He was much more open and warm with me. He wanted actually to see the transcript of my interview with his father. This, of course, I could not allow. He did caution me that his father was considered by many people to be demented, and that I should not in any way take his opinions seriously, although certainly he understood that I was likely to include them in the account. He invited me to visit a house he owned in a different part of Osaka Prefecture. I could stay for some days and obtain the rest of the information I needed. He was to be there with his wife and children for three weeks, a vacation of some kind. He could be at my disposal. This enormous change was very moving. I felt immediately that I ought to have unintentionally offended his father long before, if this was the tangible result. This first (of the second session of interviews) interview took place outdoors in a pavilion on Oda Jiro's land. The "house," as he termed it, was rather a modest estate. There were two main buildings and several small outbuildings. A creek ran through the property and there was a fine garden as well as a curated wood with a walk set through it. In short, it was a magical place, designed by Jiro himself, giving a clear indication that his sister had perhaps paid her youngest brother short shrift when she accounted him a philistine. As I said, for this first interview regarding Sotatsu's time on death row, we sat at an outdoor pavilion. Jiro's daughter, who was six, had taken a liking to me and was repeatedly bringing me flowers—these are the interruptions in the tape, which I may or may not omit from the transcript in the book proper. In any case, as you can see, even as things became grimmer for Sotatsu, I had emerged into a place of sunlight. I felt full of hope: now I truly would be able to tell the whole story of this tragic life.]

Ξ

INT.   I wonder if you could speak at all on the subject of your brother's starvation attempt, or hunger strike, as some have called it. As I understand the facts, you were unable to be in the courtroom for the trial, but you visited him during that period at the jail. Is that so?

JIRO   I visited him three or four times during the trial. My foreman at the plant where I worked had become frustrated with me and was looking for any excuse to fire me, which he eventually did. I could only manage to get time on perhaps seven or eight occasions, and on at least four of those I arrived at the jail only to be told I could not see him, that he was being exercised, fed, etc.

INT.   Do you know what these *feedings* consisted of?

JIRO   I do not. They found some way of forcing him to eat. I don't know if they used a tube or held him and forced things down his throat. I don't know. It could have been as simple as a priest with a spoon. My brother had an irrational liking for priests.

INT.   But you had seen that he was not eating? On your visits there, you had seen that?

JIRO   I noticed that he was thinner. His appearance was grim all along. At some point, he did seem very weak.

You have to remember, we were no longer speaking at this point. There had been speech at that one time, when I brought the lawyer. Apart from that, we just stood and looked at each other. When he became very weak, he would just drag himself over to the bars and sit hunched against them, letting the bars press into his back as far as they would go.

INT.   And you couldn't tell he was starving?

JIRO   You ask that now and it seems like a good question, a good clever question, but there's no cleverness in situations like this. Could his spirit have been broken? Could his mind have broken? Could his nerves have broken? Could his body have broken? Any of these things could have been the case. All of these things were likely, even. So, it isn't as clear as it sounds, not at all.

INT.   I didn't mean to suggest . . .

JIRO   Just continue.

INT.   Did you notice a change in him once they began to feed him again?

JIRO   He got more energy. He began standing again. They tell me he was carried into the courtroom on the day of his trial, that he was propped up on the chair, and that a bailiff had to stand by and keep him in it or he would fall out.

INT.   I hadn't heard that.

JIRO   But you know what I believe?

INT.   . . .

JIRO   I think that the hunger strike wasn't real. I think it was
        another tool they used to try to break him, to try to get
        him to sign another confession, confessing more.

INT.   Because the first confession wasn't enough . . .

JIRO   It wasn't enough. They wanted more from him. Maybe
        they started to starve him and he turned it around.
        Maybe he said to himself, fine, then I won't eat. Then
        I'll just die. I think he saw it as a way out. Things had
        become so bad, and there was no door. Then they
        showed him this door of not-eating.

(A minute of silence, tape running.)

INT.   And there would be no way to know, to know which it
        was.

JIRO   No way, a hunger strike imposed by the guards on a
        prisoner who won't break would look identical to a
        hunger strike staged by a prisoner as a protest. No one
        could tell the difference.

INT.   But in this case they didn't want to starve him to death.
        They wanted to execute him.

JIRO   Right, so they had to make him eat.

Interview 11 (*Watanabe Garo*)

[*Int. note.* Through a very peculiar and wonderful action of chance, the landlady who rented me the property on which I conducted many of the interviews had a friend whose brother had worked in the prison where Oda Sotatsu sat on death row. Apparently the high profile of the case had led to this brother's stories of Oda becoming common anecdotes that were told and retold in that family, eventually reaching the ears of the landlady to whom I came. When she learned what I was writing about, she put me in touch with the brother. I spoke to him several times on the telephone and once in person at a ramen house in Osaka. He was an extremely vain man in his sixties and he boasted at every conceivable opportunity. Even the ramen house we met at, it was a *personal connection*. He would get us some kind of special service, he said. In fact, they did not know him at all. It is my belief that this man did not personally know Oda Sotatsu at all, but rather that he relayed all manner of prison lore and anecdotes about Oda Sotatsu, casting them in the first person as though he were the one having had the experiences. As anyone familiar with oral histories will attest, this is quite a common occurrence. His narratives of the time are quite compelling, however. Whether that is because he actually knew Oda, actually was there, or whether it is due to him repeating the anecdotes countless times, I can't say. However it may be, he was an invaluable source of otherwise unobtainable data about this time period and I am grateful that he consented to speak to me.]

[This first interview occurred via telephone. The house in which I lived (the leased property) had no telephone, so I made use of the telephone situated on the property immediately adjoining.]

☰

INT.   Hello. Mr. Watanabe.

VOICE   One moment. Garo! One moment, please.

(Noise of the phone being put down.)

(Perhaps thirty seconds.)

(Noise of the phone being picked up.)

GARO   Mr. Ball.

INT.   Thank you for taking the time to speak with me. We are being recorded at this time.

GARO   I understand.

INT.   You were a prison guard at the L. Facility during the spring of 1978?

GARO   I was employed there from 1960 to 1985. Yes, you could say . . .

(Laughs.)

GARO   You could say I was there in 1978.

INT.   And you were a guard on what is called death row, with the most dangerous prisoners?

GARO   The ones on death row aren't always the most dangerous; that's what people often think, but it isn't always true. Quite the opposite sometimes. Certain types of assault, certain types of fraud, in-house kidnapping, what is that called in English?

INT. Home invasion.

GARO Yes, home invasion, or rape and mutilation. These are all crimes that don't get you too much time. But the guards know. We know which ones to watch out for.

INT. You learn that?

GARO I think you just know it. If you don't, you don't last long. So, it takes care of itself. In the long run, you get guards who know what they're doing.

INT. You met and dealt with Oda Sotatsu at that time? The man convicted of the Narito Disappearances?

GARO Sure, I dealt with him. If walking back and forth, looking at him, talking to him, bringing him food, counts. I only spoke to him three times. Three times in the eight months he was there. And he liked me. He wouldn't speak to anyone else.

INT. Eight months? I was told he was on death row for only four months.

GARO Not to my knowledge. Four months is awfully short, awfully short. Don't think I've heard of that. Matter of fact, eight months is short for a capital case. Almost unheard of. We used to say someone must have wanted him dead for it to come so quick, his number to come up, I mean. Seems he skipped clear to the head of the line. Supposedly he had an enemy, some minister, didn't like how things went, wanted an example, I can't say. He was easy, though. Tell you that much. Made no trouble, not once.

(Something indecipherable.)

INT.   I'm sorry, I couldn't make that out. What did you say?

GARO   I said he was so good they let a girl in his cell, right before the end. Not that he knew it was the end, mind you. Execution's always unannounced. Never know. They drag 'em off through a series of rooms, one after another. We called it visiting the Buddhas because there are different statues, one in each room.

INT.   I have questions about that, but first . . .

[*Int. note.* Here we lost the connection. It was a couple of weeks before I managed to speak to him again. That continuation will come shortly.]

Photograph of Jito Joo

[*Int. note.* Watanabe Garo gave me a photograph that he claims had been in Oda Sotatsu's death row cell. When I later met with Jito Joo, she admitted having given it to him. This strengthens Watanabe's claims of having known Oda; it is also possible he recovered it from another guard, or from the cell, without having known Oda. Further conjecture on the exact degree of his reliability is likely useless.]

Interview 12 (*Brother*)

[*Int. note.* This was somewhat later in the same conversation at the pavilion. Jiro and I had been drinking, and he had begun to tell me some stories from his and Sotatsu's childhood.]

Ξ

INT.   So your father refused to take you along on the fishing boat?

JIRO   He said it would be bad luck for me to come.

INT.   And why was that?

JIRO   He said it had to do with my birth date, that it was not an, what did he call it, not an auspicious day for a fisherman to be born. He wouldn't even let me on the boat when it was out of the water.

INT.   But he would let Sotatsu?

JIRO   Yes, Sotatsu went with him on many occasions.

INT.   Did that divide the two of you? Did you feel that you were in some kind of competition for your father's esteem?

JIRO   No, not at all. I have heard of families like that, certainly, but . . .

(*Laughs.*)

JIRO   . . . not in the least. If anything it was always Sotatsu and me together against the rest of them.

INT.   You two had a special trick you would do, right? At school?

JIRO   Yes, sometimes Sotatsu would throw a stone through the window of my classroom. Then the teacher would go off trying to find who had done it and the class would end early. I also did this for his class.

INT.   But how did you manage to not be in school at that time?

JIRO   I would be using the toilet. Or, I would say so.

INT.   And was he ever caught doing this?

JIRO   He wasn't. I did get caught, though, several times. As a matter of fact, I don't think I ever got away with it. The schoolteachers were always suspicious of me, I don't know why.

INT.   Do your own children take after you in that respect?

JIRO   How do you mean?

INT.   Well, that one seems to be trying to run away with my hat.

JIRO   Yes, nothing is safe around here.

Interview 13 (*Brother*)

[*Int. note.* Shortly after that, I asked him about his father's reaction when he discovered that Jiro was still visiting Sotatsu. He had told me earlier that his father had been angry, but he hadn't gone into detail. Later, when I asked again, he was more forthcoming.]

☰

INT.   How did it come about that your father learned you were visiting Sotatsu?

JIRO   There was a photograph, an unfortunate photograph that was published in the newspaper, a photograph of the prison. Some photographer had visited there to take photographs of various inmates, my brother included. He passed me at the prison entrance and noticed my resemblance to Sotatsu. I tried to avoid it, but he took my photograph and sold it to the newspaper. He sold a photograph of me visiting my brother for money, and that photograph was seen by my father. He demanded that I come to see him. I did so. He was furious. He said that a decision had been made and we would all stand by it. He said that some of us were trying to continue to live, to continue with our lives, and that I wasn't making anything easier for anyone. I replied that, in fact, I was. I was making things easier for myself and for my brother, Sotatsu. I told him that I didn't believe Sotatsu had done anything wrong. I said I didn't like any of it from the beginning to the end. He said that I was still stupid, and had always been so. That whether Sotatsu had done something or not was not the point and never had been. He said that you had a chance with each life, each person's life, that there was a chance to get along without drawing the wrong kind of attention to yourself. That if you did, it was never good, it always ended badly, and the facts of the matter were nothing, were no good. He said I had a liar's respect for the truth, which is too much respect.

INT.   And that's when he . . .

JIRO   He told me he didn't want to see me again.

INT.   But he went back on that.

JIRO   He did. Later that same year he went back on it. But he was so changed then that it didn't matter. He was a different person. As he is now. You can see, can't you? There's no satisfaction to be had from the person you met.

INT.   . . .

JIRO   Whether you will say so or not, you can see what a shell he is.

(Tape clicks off.)

Interview 14 (*Watanabe Garo*)

The First Time He Spoke with Oda Sotatsu

[*Int. note.* This was the interview at the ramen house, and it was the interview to which Garo brought the photograph I showed some pages back. He had the photograph in a manila envelope along with other things that he did not show me. I was very curious about what else was in the manila envelope, but if it was perhaps necessary for me to have won his trust further in order to have seen it, then in that case I failed to do what was necessary. I did not learn of the other contents. The photograph that he did give me, that of Jito Joo in a kimono, had writing on the back. The writing read, *On a lake, they float, but they do not see the lake. They only see what's above, and only in the day, and only when the sun is not too bright.* I tried to discover the provenance of those lines but was unable to, until speaking to Jito Joo herself. For now, however, I was sitting opposite Watanabe Garo in the ramen house, my tape-device dwarfed by two enormous bowls of ramen.]

☰

INT.   I am very curious, of course, to hear anything you might have to say about Oda Sotatsu, but most of all I'm curious to hear about the times when he spoke to you. Do you remember which was the first time?

GARO   Do you think I could forget a man like that?

INT.   So, he made a powerful impression, visually?

GARO   No, no, not at all. In fact, that was the thing that was most fascinating. When you were in a room with him it was like you were alone. He had the least presence of anyone I have ever met. It wasn't just that he was quiet. Of course he was, that was his thing, no? But also, he simply appeared to be elsewhere.

INT.   And where do you think that was?

GARO   Some of the guys used to say they would wring it out of him. There were those who didn't like him, I guess. We were divided along those lines. The newer guys didn't like him. The older ones just valued behavior above everything.

INT.   So, the older ones liked him?

GARO   Yes, yes, we liked him.

INT.   And the first time you spoke to him, what circumstance was that under?

GARO   It was about a shogi set.

INT.   A shogi set?

GARO   Most of the prisoners awaiting execution, or appealing it while waiting, they get a shogi set.

INT.   So, they play with each other? Or with the guards?

GARO   They do not play. Not with each other, and not with the guards. They mostly just move the pieces around. Some of them like to act like they are playing games by themselves, but I don't think they really do. I think they just move the pieces to pass the time.

INT.   But, presumably some of them do know the game and can play by themselves.

GARO   I think they know how to play. I just think it is useless to play by yourself. I have watched them doing it. It isn't really a game, not like you would think.

INT.   So, you were bringing him a shogi set?

GARO   When he spoke? No. He had the set. He would always take the gold generals out of the set and hold them in his hand. I don't know why. So, it became this question. Why did Oda Sotatsu hold on to the gold generals? A reporter was visiting and noticed. She noticed too that the pieces on the board were set up strangely. It became this thing—everyone was wondering, was this a clue? Was he finally revealing something about where the victims were?

INT.   So, the press was just allowed into the prison?

GARO   Rarely. Hardly ever. Really not much at all. This was an exception, I'd say. Anyway, so there was a bet. I don't remember what we bet, maybe some portion of our salary or shift pick or something. It did matter, though. Oh, now I remember. It was vacation. The one who bet right would get a day of the others' vacation. There was a lot of talk. But, Oda wouldn't explain. He wouldn't say why he was doing it. Different guards

S
I
L
E
N
C
E

O
N
C
E

B
E
G
U
N

came up to him, asking him. They threatened him, they begged him. Nothing worked.

INT.   But you got him to explain it?

GARO   Well, I just noticed it by accident. He was using the board as a calendar. To do that, you only need thirty-six pieces, not forty. So, he would take the gold generals off the board. I don't think he liked them being on the floor of the cell, so he would hold them. It was as simple as that. I noticed because I saw that he changed the board first thing when he would wake up. Nobody else knew what that meant, but eventually I did. So, I said to him, *Prisoner Oda, you missed a day.*

INT.   "You missed a day"?

GARO   That's what I said, *You missed a day.*

INT.   And what did he say?

GARO   For a second he looked very carefully at the board. I think he was worried someone had moved it around while he was sleeping. Someone did do that once. He was checking to see that it was right. Then he said, *No. I didn't miss any days.*

INT.   And that was it?

GARO   That was it. It got me two weeks off. That's probably why I was so nice to him from then on. That and the fact that . . .

INT.   That what?

GARO   That it made me feel good he would talk to me and not
        to the others. I liked to pretend it was because I had
        secrets, about how to be a guard, but it wasn't that.

INT.   Who can say?

Interview 15 (*Brother's Wife*)

[*Int. note.* I spoke to Jiro's wife one of the days when I was enjoying their hospitality. She was a very sharp and argumentative woman if she felt she was right, and we got along quite well. In the evening time, the family played various games, board games and games of other sorts, and she was merciless. I played her in go, a game at which I can claim little skill, and she defeated me with very little effort. She seemed to be glad that I was writing this book, and that I was meeting so often with Jiro. One morning while I was sitting out very early (I had been unable to sleep), she came out and sat by me and we spoke. I didn't record the conversation, but I remember a good deal of what she said. I paraphrase below.]

≡

She said that I should know, that Jiro wouldn't say all of it, but that I should know that Jiro's family has not ever been any good to him, not in the least. That even now all they want is for him to give them money. They don't even want him to visit. She said that his sister is the worst of all, a petty intellectual. She said that one of the great sadnesses in her life is that she didn't get to meet Sotatsu, as Jiro speaks so highly of him, and that she just knows, just knows that they would have been very close. When I asked if she had known about the Narito Disappearances and the whole business when she met Jiro, she said that she had. She said that there was no getting away from it. But, she said, it hadn't made her think any one thing more than another. Maybe it would for some people, but not for her. I asked her if they often saw the rest of the Oda family. She said she discouraged it as much as she could, and that I could print that, if I wanted to.

Int. Note

[I went on a walk with Jiro on one of the days I visited there. He said there was a way to go that would be quite pleasant, especially on a day like that. I didn't know what he meant. It seemed like any other day, but when we went outside, there was a sunshower going on. He said he loved sunshowers more than any other weather. They were good luck, but some people said you shouldn't go out in them. Do you go out in them? I asked. I always do, he said. Always. We went down off of his property and along a thin road. No cars came or went. He told me that you get the whole place to yourself, since everyone stays in. Which place? I asked him. Any place, he said, laughing. After a while, we passed a small wooded area with some broken-down buildings. They were a deep rust red, and there was old broken farm equipment here and there. Something that had been a barn was now leaning on itself, huddling in. The site was quite arresting. I said there was no good catalog of the human qualities of buildings or alleys. Jiro asked me what I meant. I said something like, there is a quality of firmness or importance, secret importance that one puts on small geographies and features of landscape, houses, yards, hidden spots beneath trees. To have a list of such places. That was my explanation, and it prompted him to tell me the following.]

☰

JIRO   Is it on? All right. This is the memory. When we were
        boys there was an old gate at the end of a little road.
        We would go to it. Do you know what I mean? Do
        you remember boys go to things, to places where
        limits exist—to the end of things wherever they can
        be found, to the bottom of holes, to the sea, to walls,
        fences, gates, locked doors. Do you remember of all

places, these are where boys feel their real work must be done? My parents had never taken us there. Matter of fact, we had never even seen anyone else on that road at all. When we stepped onto it, we felt we were gone away. Well, we would go there and look at this gate, just stare at it. We felt it was unclimbable, it was so rusty and sharp.

INT.   You went there often, you say?

JIRO   At this time, at this one particular age, we were always there. We'd sit some distance from it, and have muttered conferences, make plans. Or if I just ran off from the house, or Sotatsu did, the other one would know that that's where to go. He'd go there and find the one who'd run off. I was always finding Sotatsu there, and he was always finding me there. We thought that gate wasn't in use, that someone had closed it a hundred years before, and that no one even remembered it was there. But, one day we went there and it was open. It was half swung open and the way was clear. I was terrified. It is hard to explain how frightening it was to me. I didn't even want to go near it, but Sotatsu pulled me along. I balked at the very edge and he continued on. When I saw that he was going to go through, I started crying and ran home. I didn't look back, not once. He went in by himself.

INT.   Do you regret it?

JIRO   Somehow it happened that I never asked him what was in there. It seems like I would have, like such an important question couldn't possibly have escaped me, but that is exactly how it happens. Children are constantly forsaking whole methods of thinking in favor of new ways, and with that they give up all the old questions. Of course, later they remember. What did Sotatsu see in there? I am so fond of him when I think of it, when I imagine him at that gate, disappearing from sight. It is something I never saw, but I wish I had.

Int. Note

I went to visit the prison that Oda Sotatsu was kept in. I was not allowed to go inside, but I took photographs from the car that I had rented, and I drove to various points in the countryside where there were vantages onto it. I would like to say it was a remarkable building, but it wasn't much of anything. An ugly complex, not even particularly threatening. There was a small store about a half mile from the entrance where they sold soda, candy, newspapers, maps, etc. I asked the man what he thought about the prison. He said it kept him in business. Apparently people would buy things there to take to inmates when they visited. *What's the most popular thing?* I inquired. He held up some peculiar candy that I had never tried. I bought some of it.

I knew, of course, that it wouldn't be the same thing people had been bringing in when Oda Sotatsu was there. I knew that. But when you are dealing with something as odd as this, you sometimes get a sense for how to behave. I felt like buying that candy changed my relationship to the prison. The remaining photographs I took were a little different. Later I asked someone, a photographer friend I knew, I asked her to look at the photographs I had taken. Of the lot of them, she separated out the six I had taken after going to the convenience store.

These ones, she said, *these are much better than the others.*

Interview 16 (*Brother*)

[*Int. note.* On this day I had decided to be bold and ask Jiro about why he hadn't tried harder to convince Sotatsu to recant. However, my opportunity for such a question did not arise.]

≡

INT.   Your brother had been in the prison then for a few weeks when you finally saw him?

JIRO   That's true. The guards were confused. At first they took me to the wrong prisoner. It was an old man. He came to the edge of his cell and peered at me. I think he was trying to remember who I was. Probably no one had visited him in years.

INT.   How long did you stand there?

JIRO   Not long. I said, *Good luck, old-timer.* He called me some name that I don't remember. His voice was very shrill. The guard was looking at the paper he had been given. Suddenly he figured it out. He apologized and took me to the right place. It sounds very comedic, I know, but in a place like that, I don't think the guards would do such a thing on purpose. I believe it was a mistake.

INT.   But then he did take you to Sotatsu?

JIRO   Yes, and my brother was actually in another ward entirely. Not even the same building. In his special building all prisoners were in single cells. They couldn't see one another. They ate alone. Even the exercise,

which was walking around in a concrete atrium—
even that was alone.

INT.   How large would you say the cells were?

JIRO   Perhaps seventeen square meters.

INT.   And you were the first visitor he had had in weeks?

JIRO   I believe he had another visitor. I was told that. I think
the girl was still seeing him. She was going during
the trial, and the guard mentioned her to me. He said,
your sister has been coming. Of course, I knew that
wasn't true. She did every single thing my father told
her, everything he ever said, no matter how small,
she did that thing exactly. There was no chance that
she was visiting Sotatsu against my father's wishes.
That's when I remembered that I had seen Jito Joo
at the police station, and I connected her with a girl
mentioned in a news report during the trial, a girl
visiting Sotatsu.

INT.   Have you ever spoken to her about it, since that time?

JIRO   Never.

INT.   To get back to this first moment, the guard took you to
Sotatsu's cell. Did Sotatsu get up when he saw you?

JIRO   He was asleep. The guard had handed me off to a
different guard. In fact, that process had happened
three times. This deepest guard, he woke Sotatsu
up by banging on the door. He opened the door and
stood in it, banging it. Sotatsu opened his eyes. I could

see from where I stood, he opened his eyes but didn't move aside from that. Here was a guard banging a stick and shouting his name and he just calmly lies there.

INT.   Did you say anything?

JIRO   He sat up after a minute. When he saw me, his expression didn't change, but he came over. The guard had shut the door by then, but there was a window that slid open and we could see through it, we could still see each other. I was always trying not to blink. I would stare and stare at him and then eventually I would blink, but he never would. I stood there with him until it got dark, maybe two hours. The guard told me five times, six times, I had to go, but I had a feeling I was getting all I would get of him, that I wouldn't see him again, so I didn't want to go. I put all of myself into just watching and stood there looking at him as powerfully as I could. Eventually, I had to go. And as it turned out, I was wrong. I did get to see him again. But, I was glad I stayed as long as I could that day.

INT.   So, you left the prison when it was getting dark?

JIRO   Yes.

INT.   And you said the bus didn't stop there? You had to walk to the bus station?

JIRO   It was a two-hour walk to the bus station from the prison. Then, the bus didn't run at night, so I slept in the bus shelter, leaning on the bench and an aluminum fence, and caught the bus the next morning back in time for the second shift.

INT.   That mustn't have been so easy for you.

JIRO   It was hard, having what happened happen to him at all, but then, having him in a place that was so difficult to reach? That's why I only went to see him maybe eight times. Maybe if I had had a car it would have been easier. I could do it, though, sleeping at the bus stop, walking for hours, I could do it because I could hardly feel anything. If it was like that for me, I was always thinking, what was it like for my brother?

Interview 17 (*Brother and Mother*)

[One day, I managed to convince Jiro to come with me to speak to his mother one final time. I had tried repeatedly to get access to her again, but she would not meet me. Jiro said that he thought he could convince her, but that if his father found out, it would never come to pass. He was as good as his word, and we met her in a park. There was a little wood and two benches sitting across from each other. I put the microphone by her and Jiro. I sat on the other bench. Some of my questions turned out to be inaudible, so I have reconstructed or omitted them. The words spoken by Jiro and Mrs. Oda were entirely clear.]

INT.   I wanted to speak to you a little more, because I know that there are so many things you know that no one else does. Your knowledge of Sotatsu is something very valuable, I think, and I would appreciate it very much if you would share some more of it with me.

MRS. ODA   (nods to herself)

JIRO   We were speaking of the time that Sotatsu got a medal at school. Do you remember that?

MRS. ODA   (makes a shushing sound)

JIRO   Of course you remember that. I was trying to recall what the medal was for, but I couldn't. Do you remember?

MRS. ODA   Geometry. A geometry medal.

INT.   Was there some kind of competition that he won?

JIRO   Yes, I think there was. I think he won a geometry competition and they gave him a medal. He was very proud of it. As a matter of fact, I believe he kept it his whole life.

MRS. ODA   That's nonsense. It wasn't a competition. It was a thing he had to do, to get up in front of the school and present at a visit by the mayor. The teacher had him do it because she thought he would do the best job of it, but he didn't. He actually misdrew the shape and labeled the lines wrong. The teacher gave him the medal anyway, since it had already been made.

JIRO   He always told me . . .

MRS. ODA   The teacher was very embarrassed. I believe he left the school partway through the year and they had to find a new teacher.

JIRO   Oh, now I remember—and that was because . . .

MRS. ODA   Because your brother embarrassed us.

JIRO   I didn't know that.

INT.   But he was ordinarily very good at math, then? That was why the teacher had selected him?

MRS. ODA   I don't think so. I don't think he was good at math.

JIRO   Come now. He *was* good at math. You know that.

MRS. ODA   I don't know much of anything. Your father and I went to the auditorium. You were there too. So was your sister. We sat there and someone from each class went up to show the mayor what they were learning. Sotatsu was wearing new clothes that we had bought just for that. We didn't have very much money. Hardly any. But we did this, because we wanted to show people that we were as good as anybody. He was up there in line with the others. We sat in the audience. Practically the whole town was there. Then the mayor came in, and he went up to the stage, and he shook hands. They brought out the young students to do this and that, and they did it. Then someone showed a science project. Then someone showed something about photography, an older child. Then it was Sotatsu's turn. He was trying to show something, I don't know, something about a triangle. He drew it wrong. Everyone froze up. Sotatsu kept trying to explain it. I don't know actually if he did draw it wrong, or if he wrote the wrong numbers, but they didn't match up. He kept pointing to the drawing on the chalkboard. Meanwhile the mayor was just looking away. He wouldn't look at Sotatsu. Your father and I, we . . .

INT.   Mrs. Oda . . .

[Jiro's mother got up then and walked away, saying something under her breath to Jiro that I couldn't make out. That was the last I saw of her.]

Interview 18 (*Watanabe Garo*)

[*Int. note*. This is from a later portion of the in-person interview. It was difficult to keep Garo on subject, so much of the interview was worthless, or I should say it alternated between being invaluable and being worthless. Some subjects will not disclose information unless they feel they are in a conversation. These individuals ask questions of the questioner, beg for particulars and follow ultimately useless lines of inquiry. Such was Garo. I am therefore skipping the tedious discussion of my own life (with his interminable quizzing), as it has no bearing here. I skip to a point at which we are discussing discipline at the prison.]

≡

INT.   But there were beatings?

GARO   I'm not saying there were beatings, not as such. I'm saying if someone ended up deserving a beating, it would be a rare thing for him not to end up, one way or another, getting the thing he deserved. Do you see it? It isn't about one person deciding to discipline someone, a guard or anybody else, it isn't about that person choosing something. It isn't about the way in which such a thing is gone about. It's an inevitable thing, a person behaves again and again in a way that is a kind of communication. It is someone saying, I don't learn the usual way. Try something else with me. And eventually someone else tries something else. Talking about context, it isn't even the right way. I mean, maybe if you mean, maybe if you are talking about the difference between being above water or below.

INT.   You are talking about a guard beating someone with a
           stick?

GARO   Yes, but it isn't beating, it is communication. It isn't an
           action, not in and of itself. It's a constant pressure, the
           effect of a constant pressure. It is a result, not a thing.
           It can't be looked at by itself, separated out.

INT.   Did Sotatsu get beaten that way?

GARO   I don't believe he was ever beaten. Nothing physical, or
           not much, was ever done to him. He went along with
           things, mostly. He wasn't any trouble. And he wasn't
           there for long. Also, there is a feeling around some—
           that they are doomed. When that feeling comes, the
           guards tend to have as little as possible to do with that
           person. Most of them.

INT.   But some don't?

GARO   Well, there was one guard.

INT.   What did he do?

GARO   He would lean up against the window of Sotatsu's cell
           and he would talk. He would stand there talking to
           him for hours.

INT.   What was he saying?

GARO   Nobody knew at first, but it came out after a while. It
           was maybe a week of this guy having shifts with Oda
           and talking to him. Then a supervisor found out and
           moved the guy on.

INT.   But what was he saying?

GARO   Well, I went to Sotatsu's cell one of those days after the guy had been talking to him for quite a while. Sotatsu is sitting there on the bed, holding his shogi pieces, staring at his feet. He looks up and sees me. Something made me open the door and come in. I said, *What's the problem?* He looked at me for a little while and I stood there. Then he says, *Is it true what Mori says, the way the hanging goes? Is it really like that?* That's how I found out.

INT.   All that time he was whispering to him about the execution?

GARO   He was, and what's worse, he was just making up hideous things. Horrible things. He said they brought the family and made them all watch. He said they hanged you naked so they wouldn't have to bury the clothes. I don't know half of what he said, but it was awful. Sometimes that happens to a man in that environment. You can start doing things like that. Mori, I guess, he wasn't suited for the work.

INT.   So what did you tell Oda?

GARO   I described the hanging to him. We're not supposed to do it. Sometimes it'll spook the prisoners, make them harder to deal with. We're not supposed to, but I figured, what Mori began, I had to finish. So, I explained it to him.

INT.   Can you describe it now?

GARO   Well, this was a long time ago. I don't know how it's
        done currently. I wouldn't want to talk about that.

INT.   Can you just say again what you said to Oda about
        those hangings, the way it used to be done? It doesn't
        have to mean anything about what goes on now.

GARO   I think so, I think I can.

Interview 19 (*Brother*)

[*Int. note.* I had to return to the city briefly, and Jiro had also returned for a meeting. So, we met at a train station, before going back to his house. At the station, we had to move around to find a spot that was sufficiently quiet for the recorder. We began several times, and had to stop and move. I got into an argument with a drunk man who kept interrupting us, and this made Jiro laugh. It was in good spirits, therefore, that we began this interview.]

Ξ

INT.   You were talking about that last visit, about how they took your things away? The tape is recording now.

JIRO   I tried to bring him a little music box I had found. It was stupid, the music box, not the idea. I think it was a good idea, to bring it, only it didn't work out. They took it away.

INT.   What did the music box play?

JIRO   Well, it sounds really stupid, but you have to know— Sotatsu loved Miles Davis, especially this one record, *Cookin' with the Miles Davis Quintet.*

INT.   But surely there's no music box that plays Miles Davis . . .

JIRO   Well, maybe there is now. I don't know about that. Then there wasn't, not really. But this one, it was a little box with a mirror inside and when you opened it, it played "My Funny Valentine," which is from that record. It was very expensive, this music box. It cost me almost a week's salary. But, I thought, if it can cheer Sotatsu up just a little, then . . .

INT.   You tried to bring it into the prison, even though you knew such things weren't usually allowed?

JIRO   I did.

INT.   And they took it away. What did they do with it?

JIRO   I imagine some guard gave it to somebody as a present. I never saw it again.

INT.   And you got into trouble over it, too.

JIRO   They took me into a room and some guy yelled at me for about half an hour. I was very apologetic. Usually, back then, I was, well, hot-tempered. I had a short temper. But, in this case, I just wanted to make sure I could get in to see him. I had taken the bus; I had walked very far. I was there at the prison. If they had made me go home, it would have been pretty bad.

INT.   But they let you in?

JIRO   They did, and it was very lucky that they did. Because that was the last time I saw him.

INT.   Can you describe that visit?

JIRO   Well, they walked me in the same way as before,

as on all the other visits. I had to sign in, had to be fingerprinted. They would sometimes check the fingerprints against the others they had made of my hands. Once, the guard made a mistake and he got the wrong fingerprints out, so they thought I was some kind of impostor. But that got solved. It was the same boss guard who fixed that situation, and who yelled at me but let me go in anyway this last time. I guess he must have felt bad about the first mix-up. He didn't seem like a bad guy.

[*Int. note*. Here, Jiro's daughter ran up. She asked if we were working on the book. I didn't know that the children knew what it was we were doing. I assume that Jiro's wife must have told them. I said that we were doing some work, maybe it would go in the book. She said that she hoped it would do what it was supposed to do, in the end. I asked her what that was. She looked at her father and said that what it was supposed to do was to make a whole bunch of people feel really bad about what happened. She said they didn't feel bad enough and now it has been a long time and they have forgotten, and that it should make them remember about how they should be still feeling bad. I said that, sure, that was part of it. Jiro laughed, a sort of half-hollow, half-full laugh. He told her to run along and she did.]

INT. So, then you were brought to the cell?

JIRO Yes. It was a strange thing to visit him in jail. You get the impression that you are returning to the same moment. I'm not sure how to say it. It's as though you went away and time continued, but for the person there, it stopped. For them it has only been a moment since you left. He was there, in the same clothes, in the same position. The same light came from the bulbs. The same pallet was laid there in the same way. I had an eerie feeling about it. At the same time, I was overwhelmed, each time I saw him, with a feeling of relief, that he was still there, that nothing more had been done to him. I approached the door, the window was slid open. Sotatsu looked over, saw me, and came to the door. He had a very odd way at that time, a very odd way of holding his mouth. I think it was because he had stopped talking. Maybe if people didn't use their mouths for talking anymore, this is the way they would all hold their mouths.

INT.   Was it open?

JIRO   A little bit open, on one side. I don't remember which.

INT.   And you stood there, looking at him, the routine you two had developed?

JIRO   We did. But only for a short time. Then the guard came and asked me to leave. He didn't give a reason. I think someone else was coming in, but I don't know why. It seemed like they were clearing me away, clearing out the area. Maybe they had just gotten the news that his day was coming, and so they wanted everything straightened out. I don't know.

INT.   That was the last time you saw him.

JIRO   I remember the haircut he had, it had been done badly, so a part of his head wasn't completely shaved. When

I see him in my head, that's the Sotatsu I see. But he is standing in a street.

INT.   When you picture him, you picture him in a prison outfit, with his head shaved, but he is outdoors?

JIRO   He is in a street, and he has the box I was going to give him. But it isn't open, it isn't playing. It's just closed there in his hand.

Interview 20 (Brother)

[*Int. note.* That night, after our return, I had gone to my room to sleep, but I was still up, looking at some notes I had taken. After a while, there came a tapping on my door. I opened it, and it was Jiro. He came in and admitted that he had not told me the truth that day, or not all of it. I asked him what it was that he had held back. He told me that on the final visit, something different had happened. I asked him what it was that was different, and why he had held it back. He said it was something he hadn't shared with anyone, and so it wasn't clear to him whether he would share it with me or not, up until this evening. I asked him how that visit, that last visit, how it had gone differently. He said Sotatsu had given him two letters that he had written. He said he had those, and asked if I wanted to see them. I said, yes. I said, I didn't realize that he was allowed to write things. Jiro said that it seemed some of the prisoners were allowed that, and it seemed Sotatsu was one of them. He gave me a paper box with a little clasp on one side. I told him I would be very careful looking at them. He went to the door but stood watching me. I asked him if he wanted these documents to be kept out of the book. He didn't say anything, but stood there. Finally he said he wanted the book to be complete. He didn't want anything left out of it. That is why he changed his mind and brought the letters. I thanked him and he went off, leaving me to open the box.]

[The document (sides one and two) will follow this page.]

Document Side One: Holograph Will

Holograph Will of Oda Sotatsu. My belongings described below should be given to my family members in the following manner.

BOOKS, perhaps a dozen, on table by window __ to my sister.

my CLOTHING, old pants, new pants, shirts, socks, and others __ burned.

my FURNITURE __ given away.

my KITCHEN contents, pots, knife, etc. __ to my mother.

my RECORDS, RECORD PLAYER, __ to my brother.

my DRAWINGS, JOURNAL __ burned.

my WORM SHOVEL, FISHING POLE, TACKLE __ to my father.

my BICYCLE __ to my brother.

my SCARF __ to my sister.

my BIRD STATUES __ to my mother.

ANYTHING ELSE __ burn or give away.

. . . my rent was paid when I was taken away, but now hasn't been since then. I don't know what that means for anything.

Document Side Two: Letter to Father

[*Int. Note.* The document has been folded and unfolded many times. It appears that it has even begun to tear along some of the folds. I imagine Jiro has opened it often to read it. When I saw him the next day, the day I was to leave his house, I returned the letters to him, and asked whether he had showed this to their father. He replied that he had not. He had never had the slightest intention of doing so, nor would he. At the time of the publication of this book, Jiro and Sotatsu's father is dead (d. 2006), so he will never see the letter in this life.]

Father,

I know why you don't come to see me. You are right that this is my fault. It is a complicated thing, but also very simple. It is so simple I can see through it like a glass window. When I do that, I see you and the others and you are waiting for something. I don't know what it is, and I don't think you know either. Someone writes something because someone thinks it should be written, it should be said. So, I write this, but I don't know why it should be, just that something should be said, before this is through.

Where the house met the back gate, I used to hide things. You never knew that. Mother, Jiro, no one ever knew it. There is a hollow spot there, and I would put a thing there now and then. This is the kind of feeling I have now. I wanted you to know that I am not worrying anymore. I am not worrying now.

OS

Interview 21 (*Watanabe Garo*)

[*Int. note.* Watanabe Garo was extremely reluctant to disclose the details of the execution procedure. I argued with him for a long time, playing on his vanity, his ego, trying to get him to say the exact words he shared with Oda. Finally, only with a cash payment and guaranteed anonymity did he disclose the details.]

≡

INT.   All right, we're recording.

GARO   He was sitting there and looking at me and I was standing. I felt pity for him then. It seemed like he was affected, like what Mori said to him had changed him somehow, and I didn't want him to have to change. He hadn't been affected by things before. I wanted to let him be who he had been during his time in the prison. It was a good way for him, and I didn't want this whispering to have altered him. It shouldn't have happened, and I thought, maybe I could fix it. Maybe I could talk to him and fix it, and things would go back to being the way that they were.

INT.   Was there something you could see in the way he looked, something different?

GARO   I can just say what I said.

INT.   Please.

GARO   I said to him, I said, you don't know when it'll be. That much is true. The prisoner can't ever know the day of his execution. One day it is the day and that's that. They bring you a snack, some kind of special snack. Something nice. Then they take you out of your cell. They take you to a hall and you notice it is a hall where you haven't been before. At first maybe you think you are being exercised, or being taken to the infirmary. But, no, it is perfectly clear, this is a different section. It is a hall that is rarely used and it feels that way. You go down the hall and there are little windows and there are no bars, no bars on the windows. Outside you can see a lawn. Then you come to a door. The guard doesn't have a key. The door just opens. Someone stands behind the door all the time waiting and when someone comes, when the time is right, he opens the door. You go through it. Now you're in a semi-open space. There is a desk with a guard-sergeant. He has a lamp and a book. He checks your papers against the book. You do not have your papers. In fact, you've never seen them. But the guard who came with you has them. A doctor comes out, along with three other guards, ones you have seen before, ones who have dealt with you in the past. You are examined and the doctor and guards sign off. They are making a written statement that you are in fact you, that it is no one else but you standing there at that moment. You sign the document as well, agreeing that you are yourself. When it is done, the sergeant unlocks a door on the far side of the area. He does this once the others have left. It is a procedure. It is all a procedure. They leave; he unlocks the door; you go through. Your two guards have been exchanged for two others. They go in with you, one on each side. You are now in the first of three rooms. The execution suite is composed of three rooms. The first is a chapel. A Buddha statue is on the altar. A priest is waiting. You may have seen him before, on his visits to these very cells. He speaks to you warmly. He might be the only one to meet your eyes. He asks you to sit. There by the altar he reads to you and what he reads you are the last rites. Now you know for sure. Even if you have been pretending that it isn't so, now it is suddenly clear. Although you have told yourself some irrational story, that on the day of your execution some event of some kind will occur, and that from this event you will know it is the day of your execution, nonetheless, such an event is an invention. The guards do not wear different uniforms. You are not offered a cigarette. You do not go outside to be taken elsewhere in a covered van. Whatever event you have imagined, it is empty and meaningless. You are read the last rites, and that experience is fleeting. So soon it is over. So quickly you are raised onto your two legs. A door in the farther side of the room opens. You go through. The next room is smaller. Someone is waiting there, too. It is the warden. He is dressed very beautifully and appears distinguished, like a general. He waits until you are positioned properly. He waits. When you are standing where you should, he reaches into his pocket. He takes out of his pocket a piece of paper. What is he going to say? Even the guards are restless in this far room. What he reads is this: he is ordering the execution. He uses your name several times, pronouncing it with wonderful care, and it is like you have never heard your name before. You are to be killed by the order of someone or something. He leaves the room and the door locks. Another guard has come in. He has a bag and out of the bag he produces handcuffs. These are placed on your wrists and firmly tightened. Next he produces a blindfold. The guards

move around you as if you are delicate. They are
performing a series of operations on an object. You are
secured. Your arms are secured. Your head is secured.
The blindfold is applied to your head and face. Now you
can no longer see. The guards guide you now. You go
through a door which must have opened soundlessly,
the door beyond the warden and the second Buddha
statue. You realize you have looked at the last thing you
may ever see. If you are wild, if you have become wild,
if you become wild, it no longer matters because you
have been secured. But most are not wild. Most are led
into the room without complaint. Even with animals,
covering the eyes produces docility. The bag the guard
brought was full of docility and you feel it. The guards
have been gentle with you; they are guiding you. You
are positioned in the final room, the last room. You
feel the space of it around you. The guards touch your
shoulders and your head. They lay something over
your head, down over the blindfold. They are so gentle
with you, like barbers. It is a rope they have laid upon
your neck. The rope is laid like a stiff collar on a new
dress shirt, and made snug. Everyone is around you,
very close. Then, delicately, they remove their hands
from you, from off your shoulders, your neck, your
arms. They step away. Now it is quiet. You can feel
the rope's upward direction. Occasionally it brushes
against the back of your head. Perhaps you can guess
where you entered the room. You are doing things like
that, guessing with senses that are not operating. A
noise comes, a trapdoor has been released and you fall
through the floor as if it were not a floor, not the floor
of a room such as you have known, but the floor of a
room like a gallows. That is the last room, a room like
a gallows tree.

2___
To Find Jito Joo

Int. Note

Something about the poem that had been written on the photograph of Jito Joo was haunting me. I woke several times in the night at the house where I was staying and the image in my mind was always the same—a still lake in a country of still lakes and a bright sun overhead. There was no sound, none at all. There was no possibility of sound. I felt in it the silence that had come over my wife—that very silence which seemed to me then to have ruined my happiness, and which began the long journey that had led me here to Japan to investigate the matter of Oda Sotatsu. I felt in it too his silence.

And so I told myself—this is the heart of it. If this is a mystery, then the thing that is most mysterious is the involvement of Jito Joo. What exactly was her relationship with Sotatsu? Why was she there at the prison? For what reason was she repeatedly admitted, if indeed it was her—all those times?

I told myself, you must find Jito Joo, and if you can, then you must show her that this is a thing you understand, this silence, even if it means saying things aloud to her that you have said to no one. You must draw out from her things she has told no one. Perhaps in it there will be something—a thing that makes sense from these silences, the silence of my wife, the silence of Oda Sotatsu, the stretching on seemingly pointlessly, of life, day after day with no one to call it off.

So, I began to look for Jito Joo wherever she might be found.

Int. Note

First, I looked for her in public records, in phone books, listings of ownership, real estate purchases, deeds, and found nothing. One supposes she could easily have chosen to go by another name. Indeed, she had every reason to want to.

Jiro had no idea where she might be. He felt it was unnecessary to look for her. I hired a private investigator (of a sort) to no avail. I don't believe the man ever left his office. I began to feel it would never happen.

There is a book that I read once, a book about an Austrian huntsman. *Any Trick to Finding.* Some year of my childhood, I found the book in the children's section of the library, where it had been placed, perhaps because the title was silly. I imagine a librarian must have put it there, thinking it was not an adult book. Actually, it was written in a very ornate and mannered English by a British gamekeeper who had known the book's subject (in his youth). I might be the only one ever to have opened the book (in that library). Certainly I was the last, because I stole it and hid it under my brother's bed behind a dulcimer and a collection of broken tambourines. Where it is now, I can't say. I think that house was demolished soon after we left it. In any case, the book was quite marvelous. It tells the man's story—his childhood in a poor Austrian village, his willingness to be of use, the discovery of his special talent, his rise to a position as head gamekeeper on one then another magnificent and extensive Austrian estate. But what was his special talent? Well—he could find anything, anything at all. Somehow the man, Jurgen Hollar, had invented a system for himself that enabled him to be extraordinarily efficient in several departments of being in which most humans act with extreme looseness of endeavor. Finding things was the principal expression of his gift.

While sitting in the yard at the house of which I have spoken, the house of the butterflies (those that I had been told of, and had believed in before their appearance), the memory of Jurgen Hollar and of *Any Trick to Finding* came suddenly to me. It had been with great difficulty that I as a boy had read the book, and perhaps it was the doggedness of my approach that had so impressed it on my mind. In any case, there I was, in a Japanese garden, considering the life of a nineteenth-century Austrian huntsman. It was to such thoughts my desperation had led me.

Jurgen Hollar, it may be related—and I give this secret to you now simply out of the general kindness of my heart—could find things because he would not look for them. This is the entire point of his book. He had a very careful method of isolating and categorizing all objects that he would find in a particular area, however large that area might be, however small (however large the object might be, however small). Whether it was a long search or a short one—whether there were many objects or few, still he would follow his credo.

Therefore, imagine this: you are asked to find a spoon. You go into a room and begin on one side of the room. First you behold a sort of long shallow couch full of cushions with a table attached that extends along a wall. That is not a spoon, you say to yourself. Next you cross the wide, sloping, rounded space of the room, walking first down then up, and approach the far side, where, upon a long flat section, you see a sort of kitchen area. There is where spoons are to be found, you think. First you lift one thing then you lift another. Not a spoon, not a spoon you say. But Jurgen, had he been with you, would have looked at each thing in turn, and asked what it was. He would have looked at the couch, emptied it of cushions, and realized that it had a fine spoonlike shape. This may be the spoon I have been looking for. He would have noticed the odd spoon-ness of the very room in which he stood, and might well have identified that as the spoon for which he was looking. He did not permit the previously drawn categories of objects that had been set before him in the world to stop up his eyes and halt his discoveries.

Therefore, when the lord's son went missing one day, it was Jurgen who found the boy, secreted away, dressed as a girl in a humble village home spinning yarn, actually spinning yarn at a spinning wheel. When a favorite horse was missing, Jurgen found that a particular family, always begging in the marketplace, were mysteriously absent, and not begging for food as they always did. He went to the marketplace and asked himself, what is here and what is not here. He did not say, where is the horse.

And so, as with many lessons, we learn them and forget them and then are forced to learn them again. The time had come for me to regain my composure as a Hollarite, as a fellow who finds things by seeing what is there.

So, after two months of fruitless search, I stopped searching. I would spend my time looking through the transcripts of Oda Sotatsu's interrogations. I would correspond with his brother, Jiro. I would collect materials and take notes. I would prepare the parts of this very book as best I could.

Also, and perhaps most important, I would wander the area where Jito Joo had last been seen, and I would look at each thing I saw. I would ask myself, what is this that I see.

And so it came to pass after a month of sifting and thinking, I

came out of a shop on a street—a street I will tell you where I
had often walked!—and there she was. I recognized her from
the photographs I had seen. She was on the sidewalk; it was the
middle of the afternoon. She was holding a shabby cloth bag and
looking at a scrap of paper. That there, I thought, is the addition
of twenty years of life to the woman Sotatsu knew, the woman I
had seen in photographs. It is what she must look like—it is just
what she would look like. Never having seen this older Joo before,
I could not look for her, but being prepared to learn what things
were by looking at them—suddenly, I found her.

—Joo, I said. Jito Joo?

I explained myself poorly. She was somewhat hostile, at the very
least confused and distrustful. However, she also appeared to be
a person to whom others seldom spoke. After a little while, I won
her trust sufficiently that we went back to her house to speak. In
a phrase, she looked quite down on her luck. *To whom have you been
speaking,* she kept asking. *To whom?*

The House of Jito Joo

[*Int. note.* This portion is retold from memory, as I did not tape the interaction. You will notice the style of the text differs slightly. That is the reason.]

≡

We passed through several neighborhoods, each poorer than the one before, until we came to an extremely humble street. This one, said Joo, and led me up the steps of a converted building. Her flat was on the top floor, at the back of the house, and looked out onto a small untended patch of ground, and beyond it, a series of other ramshackle buildings running down a long slope.

Her apartment was largely empty. It appeared as if she had just moved in. How long had she lived there? Nineteen years in December.

It was strange, let me tell you, standing there in that apartment with a fifty-year-old Japanese woman I had never met, and no sense at all of what might come of any of it. She looked at me and waited.

Joo, I said, I want to ask you some things. I want to talk to you about Oda Sotatsu. I want to talk about Kakuzo. I want to speak about the poem that was written on a photograph of you. I am looking for this mystery. Not the mystery of why it happened but the mystery of how.

I will tell you nothing about it, said Joo. The person who would speak about it is gone now, gone a long time.

But what if I speak to you? I said. What if I speak about it—about this and about other things. What if I show you it would matter for you to speak. That speaking to me would matter.

She said nothing, but I drew a deep breath and continued.

Her apartment had no kitchen—just a sort of hot plate on a little counter with a sink. She put some water in a pot and set it on the hot plate.

You don't know me at all, I said, but I have a feeling that you know about something that I know.

And with that, I began.

Int. Note: Speaking to Joo in Her Home

I had never really known anyone, I said, until I met her. It was strange because—at that time I could not speak her language, and she spoke mine only poorly and with little understanding. Still we spoke furiously to each other. Every moment was a new chance to share confidences. I found myself trying to tell her every last thing I had ever seen.

This was your wife, asked Joo.

She is still alive, I said, but she isn't now my wife.

In fact, I said, I have not seen her now in a long time. And when I have, I do not know that person. For years we lived together. I threw everything to the winds and went with her where she would go. She had a child, a daughter, and we raised that child together. I no longer desired the things I had before. To be a writer, to make my way in the world—these were nothing. These meant nothing. I wanted simply to go from place to place with her, to sit anywhere with her and see what she would say, see what she saw, what she liked, see that she was glad. I felt the fullness of this new life—and I saw that what I had thought before was important was not important at all.

I sealed off a small life from the larger world, and we lived there, as glad as any people could be.

You can never have such a thing, said Joo. Not and keep it.

One day, I said, one day it happened that we had changed countries for the third or fourth time. We were living in a large city in the country of my birth and I was teaching to earn our living. It was not what I wanted; still, I did it, so we could live and eat, and so our daughter could go to school.

One day, my wife stopped speaking. She was in the bathroom, staring into a mirror, and she found something. Something was there, of some sort. I don't know what it was, but she found it, and from then on she no longer wanted to tell me anything. She would speak, to say things, here is the door key, or, shall we go to dinner, but to say an actual thing, to tell me something, anything, the desire for it was gone entirely. We would sit and she would stare into space. I would ask what she was looking at, what she was thinking. Nothing. Nothing in particular, she would say. I loved her beyond all measure. I would do anything I could think of, everything, to cheer her up, to surprise her. I banished all dark, all difficult things, from the house. I searched out all kinds of cheerful laughter and fellowship and offered them to her, one, then another, then another, then another. I found bright places in the city where we lived, and took her there, hoping. But her mood grew only blacker. She took to lying in bed and staring up at the ceiling. My dear, I would say, my dear. She would say nothing.

Our daughter was beginning to turn out into the world. She was of that age. She was seeking new things, things only for herself, and discovering the duplicity of other children. In the summers she would return to her home country, and so we sent her off as usual that June.

My wife was in such a grief, her father was passing, and I thought that was the whole of it, but it was beyond that. She had gone into herself in search of a whole new enterprise and she began intricate new dialogues with imagined speakers. She was a magnificent writer, one of the finest I had ever met, and she lacked for no form of invention. Suddenly, she began to invent a new way of living entirely in her imagination. From this she shut me out completely. She was now speaking solely with the ones she had imagined. And one day it came that she sought their advice: this life she was leading with me, should she escape it?

Int. Note

I was as in love as I had ever been. Constantly at her service, I came up with a dozen new ways each day to try to divert her, to make her smile and forget her grief. But it happened that a day came when I needed to travel to another city. I was to do a reading in San Francisco, and I went there. When I left that day, I felt that there was nothing truly wrong—that our troubles were small and together we would conquer them. I felt that her grief for her father was right. It seemed to me that the girl I loved would find her way through it.

But when I came back some days later, I found her things gone from the house. She was gone from the house. On the bed was a note. *I am beginning a new life.*

I went to the airport and bought a ticket. I flew for hours, got on another plane, flew for hours. It was a great distance. When I arrived in her country, I found a bus to the city, and I took it. I found myself the next morning, walking through foreign streets to the house where I guessed she would be staying. It was a place I had never been to before.

I rang the doorbell, then. The person who came out bore only a small resemblance to the girl I knew, so much had she changed. Though it had been only three days, four days—so much had she changed.

Joo adjusted her skirt, staring at me in the dim room, and I realized I had stopped speaking. I had not been speaking for some time.

You see, I said.

She nodded.

A moment passed, and noise filtered up from the street. Someone dragging something along the pavement. The noise grew and then faded away. And all the while, Joo stared at me, waiting.

Since that day, I continued, I have learned nothing more about it. I have tried to find it in her, going there to speak to her, again and again, but she no longer knows, if she ever did, and I have sought it in myself. I do not know it either. My life has been in immense confusion. I make no choices with any sense of the consequences involved. I found myself here. I saw this poem, and it struck me that there are things you know. Maybe they are not the things I need, but they are things, and they are near perhaps to what I need. Will you say them to me? Anything anyone knows about silence. Anything you know.

Come back in two weeks, said Jito Joo.

She stood up.

Can you find this house?

I can, I said.

Then come and find it in two weeks and I will see what I can say to you.

I started to leave and Joo called me back.

You know, she said, nothing is for any reason.

She shut the door.

I went down the stairs past three broken lights and one that flick-ered. The door to the ground floor apartment was partly open and I could hear people laughing. Someone was singing and there was the smell of cooking.

This is what we bear, I thought, the nearness of other lives.

But out in the street there was a man selling batteries and he smiled at me. I couldn't understand him. He was saying some-thing, but I could understand none of it. When he saw that, he held up a handful of the batteries as if in victory. He smiled again.

I shook my head at him. No, I won't have any batteries. This actual good smile, the smile of an actual good person, fell over me. But after a moment he was gone, or I was—the street was empty and none of it remained.

Int. Note

I wanted to explain myself better to Joo. I felt that what I would receive from her depended entirely on what I could give to her, on how clearly I could explain what had happened to me. I felt I had not explained myself at all. I was sure I had done it badly. I could scarcely remember what I had said.

I wrote a letter to her, and as I was beginning it, I fell asleep at my desk.

That night, I dreamed again of Joo's lake, but now there were chattering birds flying over it. They were shrieking and chattering, but no sound came. I could feel their cries on the surface of the lake, and I wept to feel it, but try as I might, I could hear nothing.

When I woke the next day, I worked at the letter. I worked at it all day, and in the evening I went and dropped it at the building where Joo lived. There was a little box with her apartment number in it, right there in the foyer of the building. I put the letter there. A kid with a stick was leaning against a wall. He was hitting the stick against his leg and looking at me.

No one lives there, he said.

I know someone does, I said. I saw her there yesterday.

Then I'm wrong, he said. I don't know who you're looking for.

Don't touch this letter, I said. If it goes missing . . .

I started to leave, and he left too. We went out into the nighttime street at the same time. He went right and I went left. When he got outside, he broke into a trot and was soon invisible. I looked up at Joo's window, but, of course, her window was only at the back of the building. In the front apartment a light was on and people were moving back and forth, their inaccessible lives casting off something like the light that settled on them.

I felt tempted then to believe, as I always do, that the people inside were happy, that they knew things I did not know, but I thought no more about it, and went home to my own cold room, and I thought of the letter I had written to Jito Joo.

Int. Note: Letter to Jito Joo

Dear Jito Joo,

Please ignore everything I said yesterday. Allow me to explain it in a different way. I have not spoken of it really to anyone, and so it came out wrong. What I said was perhaps closer factually to the way it happened, but I can say it in a way that you may understand better, in a way of immediate understanding. Let me give you that now.

A man fell in love with a tree. It was as simple as that. He went into the forest to cut wood and he found a tree and he knew then that he loved it. He forgot about his axe. It fell from his hand and he knew it not. He forgot about the village that he had come from, forgot the path along which he had come, forgot even the brave ringing voices of his fellows, which sounded even then in the broad wood as they called his name, seeking after him. He sat down there before the tree and he made a place for himself and soon no one passing there could even see that he was lying between the roots.

It was for him as though a blade of grass had turned to reveal a map of broad longing and direction and over it he could pass— and did.

He and his love then sought what they would with nothing asked of anyone. Asking no permission, they devised all manner of delights and found in each other everything that the world had lacked. You are as bright as a coin. You are as tall as a grove. You are as swift as a thought. And so well did they hide themselves in their love that grass grew over their hearts and all their loud songs became indecipherable ribbons of air.

But then one day, the man awoke. He found himself again in front of a tree, but it was one he had never seen before. He had never seen the forest either—and the clothes he wore were worn almost to shreds. Where have I been, he asked himself, and stumbled out of the woods to where others waited at a string of houses. But, they could tell him no tidings of himself.

Where have I been, he wondered. With whom, in my loveliest dreams, have I so endlessly been speaking? But as he thought it fell away, and he was poorer then than anyone.

Raise yourself up, the others called to him. Raise yourself up, you fool.

Ah, he said, so this is how fools are made. For I did never know.

++

Int. Note: Two Weeks

For two weeks, then, I wandered about in a bit of a haze. Speaking about my life had set me at an angle to the world I was experiencing. I felt in some way that I had put myself before Joo to be judged. What a ridiculous thing! Especially considering that she had done nothing to earn it. In fact, her part in the entire business with Sotatsu would lead one to believe nothing good about her. Yet, somehow, Sotatsu had trusted her, and likewise, now, I was trusting her.

I wrote several letters to people I knew back home. I tried to read two different novels unsuccessfully. I ate at several different restaurants, all of which were good, and ordered either much too much food or far too little.

In searching for a way out of my own troubles, I had found my way into the troubles of others, some long gone, and now I was trying to find my way back out, through their troubles, as if we human beings can ever learn from one another. To simply find out what had happened to Oda Sotatsu, that was the main thing. That was always the main thing. But if in learning that, I could see somehow farther . . .

Finally, after two weeks, I went back to Joo's apartment. Somehow, I expected that she would not be there, but she was. The first thing I noticed inside the building was that my letter was no longer in the box. So, she has read it, I thought. I went up the stairs. When she opened the door, she was holding the paper in her hand.

Come in, she said.

Her face was gentler than it had been. I don't know if I had won her over, or what. Her face was gentler, but in a way its gentleness revealed still further the difficulties that her life had put on her. She had the severity of a person who has lived in the out of doors, beneath a constant sun—the look of a field laborer or an Appalachian musician. I have always been partial to such faces, have always thought it would be fine to have such a face for myself. It seems there is a great deal of suffering prior to obtaining one. I thought of none of this then. What I thought then was, she is holding my letter. I was desperate to hear what she would say, about my situation, about Oda Sotatsu, about Kakuzo. Here she was: suddenly I was much closer to writing the book I longed to write, to discovering the material that would make possible the telling of the proper story.

But, the first thing she did was to go to the window and sit down. She gestured that I should do the same.

Let's not talk for a while, she said.

We sat there for a while. Through the floor, I could hear the sound of the apartment below. The sun set on some other part of the building. In Joo's apartment it became steadily darker until she was finally forced to turn on the light or leave us sitting together in darkness.

I watched her face in the light and tried to see the girl who had visited Sotatsu, who had lived with Kakuzo. After a time, I felt I could see her. She looked at me and said:

I don't think anyone has looked at me for that long in many years. This is a thing that regular people don't understand. Because they live in families or groups, because they do not live alone, unmet, they do not know what it is like to be alone. Months can go by without anyone looking at you, years, without anyone so much as touching your hand or shoulder. One becomes almost like a deer, impatient to be touched, terrified of it. A momentary contact in a supermarket, or on a train, becomes bewildering. However often such contact comes it is always bewildering, because it isn't meant. And then there comes the day when no one so much as looks at you, unless it is by accident.

She clasped her hands.

I work in the next street, at a machine company. I am a secretary. There are two other secretaries beneath me. Someone tells me what to do. I tell them what to do. It is all so simple that none of that is really necessary. I eat my lunch by myself and when work is done, I come home and sit and eat my supper alone. Sometimes I walk by the harbor and look at the ships. When you say these names to me, Oda Sotatsu, Sato Kakuzo, when you say to me this name, Jito Joo, I feel so far away. You tell me of your own life and I am sorry. You have been hurt. So have I. It isn't done. It will keep going on. I know it. But, I have read your letter. I wrote you one of my own and now you can have it. I threw it out two days ago, but then I got it back. Here it is.

She held it out to me.

I think I would like for you to go now. I wish I knew what to say to you.

She stood up. So did I.

I went to the door and she opened it.

Anything I could ever tell you, or anyone else, is in there. Goodbye.

2.1__
The Testimony of Jito Joo

Int. Note

When I got home, I opened the letter that Jito Joo had given me.
I read it straight through twice, set it down, got up to leave the
house, thought better of it, returned to my chair and read it again.

I present it to you now in its entirety.

I believe in discovering the love that exists and then trying to understand it. Not to invent a love and try to make it exist, but to find what does exist, and then to see what it is. I believe in trying to understand such love through other loves, other loves that have existed before. Many people have made the records of these loves. These records can be found. They can be read. Some are songs. Some are just photographs. Most are stories. I have always sought after love, and longed for it. I have looked for all the kinds that may be. I am writing to you now to talk about Oda Sotatsu, who is a person I loved, and who loved me. Although I know there are others who will say things about Oda Sotatsu, who may say things about me, who may know about this situation, although they are few, perhaps there are some who can speak about these things, yet what I know is what I felt and what I saw. I am not writing this for any comparison or for any other sort of understanding, but as a record of love, for use by those who love and who hope to love. I am not nimble and I cannot hide things well. I will write what I felt and how. You may see how I do.

I met Oda Sotatsu with another man, a man I was seeing, Kakuzo. It was a strange time, not a good time. I knew Oda Sotatsu hardly at all, although we grew up in the same area. I had not met him until just before he was put into prison. We had exchanged some words. The man I knew, Sotatsu, existed in his situation, as a person with no freedom. That is why I became his freedom. Others who were his family came and went and made noise. They were visiting or they were prevented. For me there were no obstacles. I do not know why that was. It seems to me that there should have been, that it was never so easy for a person to do what I did, to see a person as often, or for as many times. Why it is, as I say, I don't know. But we were lucky in that. I was Oda

Sotatsu's constant visitor, and whoever the guards were, wherever they were, I was admitted, sometimes as his sister, sometimes as a girl he knew. I was always admitted. I was never turned away, not once. There are things in life that happen like this—I can tell you that because I was there.

I was with him that night, of course. It was I who brought the confession to the police. I had a lovely green envelope. The paper was so crisp! Crisp green paper folded and secured with a string. Inside it, Kakuzo had put the confession. We were there in the night, awake, Kakuzo and I. We had parted with Sotatsu at the bar, and now we were at home. Neither of us could sleep. He was sitting there in the dark holding the confession in its envelope. There was no clock. We just sat, watching the window. Sometime after dawn, he handed it to me. He said, *Joo, take it now.* I put on my coat, went to the door, put on my shoes, and went down the stairs. Outside, it was a very bright day. I was so full of it—I felt like the hinge of some long thing. I was turning a door in the distance. A door was turning upon me, and it was all effortless. All that weight, but I could support it. I took the confession to the station. I knocked on the door. The officer was asleep at his desk. He woke up and came over rubbing his eyes. Here is a delivery, I said. Here you go.

They didn't know what it was, so who I was, I guess, was meaningless. I went away and next I knew Sotatsu had been taken. He was in jail. He was the Narito Disappearer. Suddenly. I sat all day in the house and when it was nighttime, Kakuzo and I went and found something to eat. *Will it work? Will it work?* Kakuzo kept saying. There was a radio on in the restaurant. That's how we heard the news.

++

It seems that people think of simple ways to say things or know them, but I was always taking the long way around. My mother always teased me. You go the long way every time. I do. I go the long way. When Sotatsu was in jail one day I went to see him. Something had changed for me in the room with Kakuzo and I felt cold all over, empty as a washed bottle. But in the jail I felt young. I had no idea what I was. I asked myself that. I said, Joo, what are you, as I went along the corridor and I truly had no idea.

When I came to his cell, he was sitting facing the wall. Sotatsu, I said, it is your Joo. From then on we were in an old tale. He looked at me and it was like I had lit him on fire, like he was an effigy I had set on fire at a festival. He knew what everything meant. I knew what everything meant. I said, I am coming here every day. We have a new life.

If some say that a man and woman must live together or that they must see each other, even that they must live in the same time in order to love, well, they are mistaken. A great lover has a life that prepares him for his love. She grooms herself for years without hope of any kind, yet stands by the crevice of the world. He sleeps inside of his own heart. She dries her hair with her tears and washes her skin with names and names and names. Then one day, he, she, hears the name of the beloved and it yet means nothing. She might see the beloved and it means nothing. But a wheel, far away, spins on thin spokes, and that name, that sight, grows solid as stone. Then wherever he is, he says, I know the name of my beloved, and it is . . . or I know the face of my beloved, and she is—there! And he returns to the place where she saw him, and she empties herself out—leaves herself like open water, beneath, past, in the distance, surrounding, able to be touched with the smallest gesture. And that is how the great loves begin. I can tell you because I have been a great love. I have had a great love. I was there.

++

I wore a different face, of course, when I saw Kakuzo next. He did not know what happened. He knew nothing at all. But, he told me. You keep seeing him. Keep going. I will keep going, I told him. Hold Sotatsu to his confession. Help him be brave. He is brave enough, I said. This is his myth. It is, said Kakuzo. It is his myth. I want to say how it was that I lived with Kakuzo, that I slept in his bed and woke with him, that I knew him every day and that I was not his, that I was with Sotatsu, that I was Sotatsu's, that I was in between the visiting of Sotatsu, the seeing of Sotatsu. I was in a life that occurred but once each day for ten minutes, for five minutes, for an hour, whatever we were given.

The girl Joo who went with Kakuzo where Kakuzo wanted to go, who lay with him, who sat in his lap, she was less than nothing. I set no store by her. She was a shell, a means of waiting and nothing more. Each day as I set out for the jail, I would put my life on like a garment and the blood would run out through my arms, my legs, my torso. I would breathe in and out, living, and go out, living, through the streets to my Sotatsu.

What was it for him? Some say I do not know. How could I know, they say. I never knew him. I visited. We spoke little. They say these things.

In fact, I know what it was for him. I will tell you it simply: he felt he was falling. He felt he fell through a succession of wells, of holes, of chasms, and that I was there at windows, and we would be together a moment as he fell by. Then I would rush to the next window, down and down, and he would fall past, and I would see him again.

I am not a shouter. I did not shout to him, nor he to me. We were like old people of some town who write letters that a boy carries from one house to another. We were as quiet as that.

Of silence, I can say only what I heard, that all things are known by that which they make or leave—and so speech isn't itself, but its effect, and silence is the same. If there were a silent kingdom and but one could speak—he would be the king of an ageless beauty. But of course, here where we are, here there is no end to speaking and the time comes when speaking is less than saying nothing. But still we struggle on.

I imagined once that there were horses for everyone—that it might be we could all climb on horseback and make our way somewhere not waiting for any of the things deemed necessary. I would cry at the thought—I, a little girl, would cry to think of it, but it made me so happy I can't tell you. I believe there was an illustration I had seen, in some book, of a sea of horses, and it made me feel just that—there were so many! There were enough for me to have one too, and for us all to leave.

Oh, the things I said to Sotatsu!

I said to him, I said, Sotatsu, last night, I dreamt of a train that comes once a year like a ship to some far-flung colony. I said, on the ship are all the goods that the colony needs. It carries everything, this ship, and all the colonists must do is last until the ship comes again and all will be well. Out of the west, the train, this ship, it comes along the track. It dwarfs everything. This is my dream. The gigantic train is more real than the world that surrounds it. Sotatsu, I bring nothing to you, but it is what you need what I bring and I will bring it again and again and you will wait and be strong and fare well. We will not wait, you and I, we won't wait for another life. This life, this is our life. We will have no other, nor need any other. Here all is taken care of. We have been set aside, set apart, like legs removed from a table. Our sympathies remain with each other entirely and when we lie touching, it is as though we are the whole table, as though the missing table moves back and forth between us, there where we touch, we two table legs.

I was always saying such things, and he would smile. He would turn his mouth like a person does when tying a knot or opening a letter. That was the smile that he developed in order to smile at me. I was so fond of it—let me tell you! For there were not all good times. He had lost all his strength when he was caught and it took time for him to regain it. Then he was moved and moved again. He was put on trial. He was removed from trial. He was put in a new place, and then another place, another new place.

In the first place, we soon made a routine. I would wear a coat so it could not be guessed, what I was wearing underneath. I would say, what color am I wearing? Am I wearing any color, any particular color? And he would say one color or another color, he would say a color. Then, I would off with the coat and we would see what color it was. Being wrong or right about something meaningless is very strong.

He would never guess correctly, though. I think he did it on purpose, but I don't know. Like many things, this thing I know not at all with any certainty.

I would say to him, confess to me, to your Joo. Confess that you are in love with me. Say it.

Then he would say, my Joo, Joo of the coat and colors, Joo of all visits. He would say such things, meaning that he loved me.

When we were near to each other, he would become very stiff and still. He would stare at me. I wanted to pretend that nothing mattered, for it didn't. Although it might have been pretending, if two pretend then it is no longer that. It becomes actual. I asked him to die. When he could say that he did not confess, that he did not agree with what he had said. When he could say the whole business right out, about Kakuzo, about the confession, and that he knew nothing . . . he realized, I am saying, he realized, because his brother came there and said it, he realized he could say that, and it would free him. But that same night, I was there with him, and he told me, and I said,

The line of trees that is at the horizon—they are known to you. You have not been to them, you have only seen them from far away, always for the first time. One looks out a window into the distance, or comes down a circling drive, turns a corner. There in the distance, the tree line, all at once. It is dark here and there. It moves within itself, within its own length. It is merely a matter of some sort of promise. One expects that the forest there is nothing like anything is, or has been. I will go there, one thinks, and enter there, between those two trees.

Sotatsu, I said. I am those two trees. We are entering that forest now, and the way out has nothing to do with anyone. You should not bother with anyone. They are just rasping stones that pull at you. Each person chooses his life from all the roles in all the theaters. We are a prisoner and his love. For I am sometimes one and sometimes the other. You are one and then the other. We are diving in the thin and wild air, as if the spring has just begun. We are diving but we are composing the water beneath us with our dreams, and what I see gives me hope. I will return to you, my dear, and I will return to you and return to you and return to you. You will be mine and no one else's, and I will be the same. I will turn my face away, and look at you when I am elsewhere. I will look only at you.

Then he saw that I was right, that I was the only one for him, the only one turned entirely to him, the only one looking only at him. I earned him. He knew that with that moment, there was a possession as total as any to be gained; not even the earth, consuming the bodies of our children, can have something so completely—for only I would give myself again, again, again. Our deaths we give and they are gone. But this, we give and receive, give and receive, give and receive.

✚✚

I went home to Kakuzo and I said, that brother told him to give up. He said, give up. I said, he told him to. He was going to. He said, he better not. For whom, I said. He'd better not, he said. You'd better tell him. I told him, I said. That's good. He grabbed my face and he said, Joo, that's good. You remind him.

Kakuzo was a foolish person. He was a fool, a person who is foolish as a job, as a profession. But not a fool in a court or a fool with a crowd. He was a solitary fool, his own fool. He was a fool because he did not know what made a life, and he could not see that I had made one right in front of him. He could not see the difference, couldn't see: his Joo was gone and had been replaced by a gray woman with a raincoat who nodded and sat and cooked and blinked and blinked. He could not see that it must mean this: I was living elsewhere, like the boy who stares at an old photograph and leaves his body with a sigh.

Oh, my dear! I want so much to be again in that life. Speaking of it like this, writing it down: I am like a yard of shadows when the sun is even with the lowest clouds. I am multiplied, but only with my bags packed, only where I stand, at the station, my hat pulled low. Have you seen an old woman like me? I have been old a very long time.

++

How can I explain it, put it in a line for you? I can say there were a series of visits. I can number them and recount them one by one. I do not remember any of them. That's true. Also, I remember every one without exception. It is most correct this way—I can say a thing about that time and know if it is true or not true. Then I write it down. I leave the false things on their own.

In the first part of my life with Sotatsu, he lived in a cell in a jail where the sun came south through the window on an avenue all its own where it was forced to stoop and stoop again until when it arrived at its little house it was hardly the sun at all, just a shabby old woman. Yet we were always looking for her, this sun, when she would come, always eager to have her meager presents, her thin delineations. I would say, oh, Sotatsu, oh my Sotatsu, today you are like a long-legged cat of the first kind. He would smile and laugh, meaning, Joo, I have nothing to do with such a cat as you describe.

In the first part of my life with Sotatsu, he lived in a basket on the back of a wolf that was running westward. I was a flea in the wolf's coat, and had all the privileges of my grand station. I could visit the prisoner. I could speak to the prisoner. I made the wolf aware of his important profession. I said to the wolf one day, actually, I said, you are carrying a most important prisoner, you know, away beyond the frontier. He said, flea of my coat, it is your work to tell me such things, and mine not to listen.

In the first part of my life, I told Sotatsu everything about myself. I told him I was the youngest of fourteen children (a lie). I told him I had a dress that I wore as a child with a fourteen-foot train and the other children would carry it, so becoming I was. I told him I had a course in fishing where seven would stand in a stream using fourteen hands to weave a rope and the fish would leap up and into the canvas bags we wore on our waists. Every lie was a lie of fourteen. I wanted him to know about me. I said what was true also. I said, I have seen nothing that was worthy of me until you were lying in this cell. I said, I am not my surroundings or my fate and you are not who anyone says. I said, I will say things and you can stop me, but no one else can. I will be a speaker and I will speak on all subjects like a tinny radio rustling in a shop window. I will make up all the world's smallest objects and doings. I will confuse them, muddle them like a jar, and produce them at odd times. This will be the tiniest edge, the tiniest corner of our love: so much you have yet to expect from me.

In the first part of my life, I knelt by the bars of a cell where my love lay and I called as a woman calls to pigeons when she is old and cannot see them. I made shooing noises with my mouth, for I was sure someone said once, someone said such noises would make birds come to you.

I draped myself on the bars like a blanket. I cried for him. I smiled and laughed. I was a playhouse of a hundred plays where there are no actors to do any but the one play, that first play, made when the theater, unbuilt, is first considered. If we should have a theater, this is the play we would do, and all we would need is one actor and a cloth for her to place before her face. I placed so many cloths, and taught my Sotatsu all manner of things that no one knew, not me or anyone. These were true things in our life, but empty in the common air.

In the first part of my life, I was stopped on the steps of the jail by a woman, my mother, who said she had heard about where I was going, heard about who I was seeing, heard strange things that she would learn the truth of. This woman, my mother, when she stopped me on the steps of the jail, I felt I was in a history of classical Greece, and she was my deceiver. Good mother, I told her. A person visits a friend and is unchanged.

In the first part of my life, I was asked to appear in an old film by an early director. This was filmed many years ago, he told me. You are just right for the part. There will be many scenes that are nighttime scenes, but we film those during the day, for we need all the light that can be mustered. We need as much light as possible to see, because we must be clear. We can afford for nothing to be hidden.

The first part of my life came to an end when Sotatsu was moved to the jail where they would starve him.

++

In the second part of my life, as you know, dear friend, my Sotatsu was starved almost absolutely to death by the guards who would give him no food. They said to him, you must ask us for your food. He told me, they say I must ask them for the food. I said, you? You? Ask them for food? He agreed that he would never do so. I am not in charge of my life that way, he said. He said all this by smiling. I said all this by winking. I stood at the cage in my coat and held the bars with both hands. I could see he was very hungry, and thinner.

In the second part of my life, my Sotatsu was thin almost to breaking. He had become like the edge of a hand. I wanted to tell him to eat, but I did not. Instead, I began also not to eat. I said, I will also not eat, but I was not as strong as he. When the dizziness started, and it became hard for me to rise, I knew: I would fail him. Even if I was with him in not-eating, I would be failing in my visits. I could no longer visit him, with such strength as would be remaining. So, I took to eating again, just enough, and visiting.

They would drag him off to a trial. The trial had begun and they wanted him to say things, so they were starving him and speaking to him, examining him, telling him things, asking for his signature. His hands were trembling even when they lay still. His eyes were open—they had stopped closing, I suppose this happens when one doesn't eat. Finally, it was enough. They brought him food and he began to eat. Even once they were bringing it, though, he could not eat it. His throat had forgotten its purpose. The food just wouldn't go in. So, it had to be retaught and this took a few days.

In the second part of my life, my love was rescued from starvation by a series of bowls of food. I did not ever see him eat. Such things were not allowed. But, I saw him standing one day. I arrived in the morning, quite early, and he was standing when he could not stand for weeks.

My dear, I called, my standing dear. How well you stand.

He looked at me and explained it, that he had begun to eat once more. That he had broken them. The trial was over, too. I knew that, and I was glad of it. I had the newspapers in stacks. I read them over and over. I had found the place where he would be on the map, and looked up the route.

My dear, I told him that last time, I will join you in the new place.

That was the end of the second part of my life.

++

In the third part of my life, I traveled to a prison that was built underground in order to avoid the moon. Jito Joo was the name I would give, and they would allow me to climb through a narrow aperture. They would show me into a hallway and down a hallway. They would show me to a roped-off area, where little rooms knelt like parishioners, each one bending its head. When the guards pulled a lever, the rooms would open, as many as they liked, or as few. I was allowed to go in, suddenly. I who had never been allowed in, I was suddenly allowed in. Sotatsu was sitting on a pallet. He was staring at his hands. He did not look at me. This was the first time I had seen him, I think, in my entire life, such was my feeling. I said, I am looking at him and he is here. He looked up, hearing my voice, and I sat there by him, my arm brushing against his side and shoulder.

Where will we go?

In the third part of my life, I practically lived in the cell with Sotatsu. Properly speaking, I, of course, was far away, mostly. I was mostly on the bus, going to the prison, on the bus leaving the prison, in the house with Kakuzo, sitting, eating, walking on the streets of our village, muttering greetings. I was mostly carrying on that way. But still, as I say, I practically lived in the cell. Every chance I got, I snuck away there. I was like a child with a hiding place. Where is Joo? Where has Joo gone? Joo may be found in the death cell of a prison with her beloved.

I believed then that the third part of my life was my whole life. I had forgotten about the two previous parts. I did not expect a fourth. I believed we would continue that way. Everyone on death row had been there always. They were very old. They expected to die of natural causes and be given neat Buddhist ceremonies attended by whatever gentle family members remained. In this we encouraged them, the guards encouraged them, the guards encouraged us. We were all sternly encouraged in the belief: the world would last forever.

194

SILENCE ONCE BEGUN

Sotatsu, I would say, some speak of the great cities of the world where anything can be bought. These are the sorts of things I would say, and he would laugh. We would sit, laughing, like old campaigners. (I have known a few, and we are not like old campaigners, he would say by smiling, and I would say, you have known no old campaigners but we are old campaigners of a certainty.)

The third part of my life was where I was told the meaning of my life. One knows the weight of a thing when it is strong enough to bear its own meaning, to hear its own truth told to it, and yet to remain.

Sotatsu, I said, I am your Joo. I will come here forever and visit you. All I need is a small profession, just enough money for the bus and for food. I need no children, I need no objects. I need no books, no music. I am a great traveler like Marco Polo, who visits an interior land. I travel deep into the heart of a place between walls, built between the walls of our common house. I am an ambassador, an embassy sent to a single king. You are that king, my king, my Sotatsu.

Then, he would hold up his hand as if to say, such wild notions do very well, but we must be careful.

Or—let us throw even such caution as this to the winds. Let us be like all the cavalry of ten armies.

These expressions of his, they made me wild! I would leap to my feet and sit again. The guard would come running, thinking he was wanted for some small thing, a glass of water or a query.

No, I would say, it's only that Sotatsu made a joke.

Then Sotatsu would look at his feet, which, predictably, were doing the things that feet do.

In the third part of my life, I came to a far place. I decided that I would move into a room near the prison. I decided that I had enough put away, that I could do that. I was planning it. I did not tell Sotatsu. I came the night I decided it, and I was allowed in very late. I have told you there were no obstacles and it was always true. No obstacles. I appeared and was admitted. I was taken to his cell, and the guard shut the door. He pulled a shade. I didn't know the shade was there, but he pulled it, and the cell was closed off. It could no longer be seen from without.

Hello, my Sotatsu, I said, and I went to him. It was the last of all my visits, and the longest. When I left the sun was halfway up in the sky. The bus had come and gone. There were no more buses that day, but one came. An empty road stretching in both directions. Then, the friendly nose of a bus drifting along. The bus driver said, you are lucky, young lady. There are no buses in this direction, not until tomorrow. I just happen to have gotten lost. Then he took me back in the direction of Sakai.

I felt when I left that day that I would return immediately. I would wait for the sun to set and then I would set out. I would be back again and pressing the buzzer, being admitted through the steel doors. I would be called upon to empty my bags, to leave my things and go past a thousand tiny windows with their attendant eyes. I had grown so used to these things that they calmed me. I looked forward to them as a series of gestures. I felt surely that nothing could take them from me. That any of it could or would end. It seems silly, but I did not believe it. Neither I nor my Sotatsu: we did not believe it.

This is a letter about Sotatsu who was my love; this is a letter about my one true life, which consisted of three parts. I am now in the fourth part of my life, and it has been false. It has been a false portion. In my estimation, they give you the false portion last.

3__
Lastly, Kakuzo.

Int. Note

Kakuzo, Kakuzo. Sato Kakuzo. In all my research, I had come upon him again and again only to hit upon one impasse or another. I felt that I must find him if I was to have the full story. As luck would have it, I managed to, but last of all, and only after a long search, culminating in a great piece of luck.

Here is how it happened:

A person like Sato Kakuzo—I imagined he could not be found unless he wanted to be found. The question then was: how does one make him want to be found? Or how does one make him reveal himself? I had a sense of Kakuzo's vanity. I felt he was not a nihilist—and that he did truly believe in history, in a parade of history. I felt surely that he would not like the idea of a faulty account, of any faulty account. And if there was to appear somewhere a faulty account of him most particularly—or of something he had had to do with . . .

I was sure that Kakuzo would want the story to be correct; after all, there was every indication that he was the original architect; it was he who wrote the confession.

So, this is what I did: I arranged with a newspaper friend to print a remembrance article about the Narito Disappearances in a Sakai paper. I purposefully left him completely out of it. A long article about the most important event of his life—and no mention of Sato Kakuzo. My friend was understandably hesitant to print such a thing, but finally he did.

For a week we waited. One day, then another. I grew afraid that he had died, or that he had been living abroad for decades. Or perhaps he simply hadn't seen that newspaper? Perhaps he hated newspapers. When a week had passed, I felt sure he would never be found.

Yet the ruse worked. A week and a half after the first article, the office of the newspaper received an indignant letter. What fools they were, the letter said, to print absolute fallacies without any reference to the truth. Were they journalists or not? Once upon a time newspapers had had a relationship to truth. Had this commitment been completely effaced? And on and on in this fashion. The letter was signed, Sato Kakuzo, and on the envelope was written a return address.

I contacted him then, and he agreed to meet.

The place of our meeting was a sort of boathouse and cafe at the shore. He showed up very late, more than an hour. I was preparing to leave when a car pulled into the lot. Indeed, it was he. Kakuzo wore an old fisherman's hat, a tweed jacket, and corduroy trousers. He appeared a perfectly innocuous older man. His English was clear and unaccented. He had brought things with him, things for me. If I were to do the story, he would have me know the whole of it.

This interview was the only time I was able to meet him. However, the materials that he gave me provided many hours of study, so I felt that I had spent a great deal more time with him than I actually ever did. One thing that must be stressed is the immense force of personality possessed by Sato Kakuzo. I left the interview unsurprised that he had made Oda Sotatsu sign the confession. Indeed, he might have managed to convince anyone to do the same.

Interview (*Sato Kakuzo*)

[*Int. note.* At first we sat at a table by the window, but the position of the sun shifted, and it became too bright, so we were forced partway through to move to another table. Both times Kakuzo chose the chair he wanted and sat in it, without seeing whether I had an opinion on the matter. I suppose, as he was being interviewed, there is a certain justice to that. It was interesting to see that he always chose the seat from which one might observe the door. When I asked him whether I could use my device to record the conversation, he refused. Only after we had spoken for a little while did he relent.]

Ξ

INT.   So, you had been inspired by the French Situationists? You were inspired by the '68 riots? That's what got you into trouble at first in Sakai and led you to return home?

KAKUZO   Do you know the fable of the stonecutter?

INT.   No.

KAKUZO   It is an old fable, Persian, I think. I had read it around that time, and it made me feel, somehow—as though certain things might be possible. I felt that things I had thought should be classed impossible were truly possible, with the very greatest effort.

INT.   What is the fable?

KAKUZO   A king is out riding with his nobles, all ahorse the very best steeds that can be had. They are riding out beyond the city where the king lives. They pass through fields and down road after road. The horse the king is riding is a fine new horse, such a horse as he has never possessed, and so he gives it its head, and the horse carries him farther than he has ever gone. The king and his nobles ride so far and so fast that they become bewildered, but their blood is in their faces and their hearts are beating so tremendously that they want only to course on and on. A wind is blowing and the weather is spinning in the air, clouds turning like looms. The horses trail to a stop, and the company is on a road before a lowly dwelling. It is a stonecutter's hut. The king dismounts, and goes to the door. He knocks and the door is answered by an old man with pale cruel hands of sinew and bone. The old man welcomes the company and receives them into his hut. Strangely enough, there is a place for everyone. The table is large enough for all. Each lord sits at table, shoulder to shoulder, and the king sits at one end. The stonecutter sits at the other. I will feed you, said the stonecutter, but it will not be anything like what you eat. The nobles groused, saying they would like this or that, saying is there this or that, but the stonecutter looked at them and they looked at his hands, and they fell silent. The king spoke, saying, they were come like beggars, and were glad to be received at all. Such a thing a king had never said. So, the stonecutter went into his larder and brought out a goose that resembled a girl. He brought out a deer that resembled a boy. He brought out bread like the hair of a hundred court ladies, threaded into rope. He brought out honey like the blood of goats. Do not eat this food, the lords said, but the king laughed. The stonecutter watched them speaking, and the king laughed, saying, where you are brought by a swift steed is a place for courage. But the lords said beneath their breath, some steeds are too swift. Then the plates were filled, heaped nearly to the ceiling and passed around, and always the king chose first, and he filled his plate and ate of it, and filled it and ate of it and filled it and ate of it. Never had he tasted such food. And soon they were all fast asleep, and the stonecutter rose from the table. That is the end of the first part.

INT.   What is the second part?

KAKUZO   Do you want to hear it?

INT.   I do.

KAKUZO   The king wakes the next day, and he finds that he is the stonecutter. He sees no lords in his house. There are no horses in his field. There are only the remains of an enormous feast, which ended sometime in the night. He looks down at his hands and he sees how terrifying they are, sees the white bone, the sinew, that which the stone may not resist. But he is a king. He sets out on the road toward his kingdom, and follows the trail of the horses' hooves. For nineteen days he walks. It takes him nineteen days to travel what on the fastest horses took a single flight of restless speed. Still he perseveres, and on the nineteenth day, he reaches the gates of his city. He presents himself there, and the guards will not let him in. Have you nothing to sell, they ask. Have you no money with which to buy? For what reason do you want to enter this fine city? Do you not know, they asked. Do you not know that this is the richest and wealthiest city in the world? And some fear in his heart keeps the king from revealing himself. I will see, he says, how the land lies. And he goes a short distance into a desolate field, and he finds a stone. He sits by the stone and passes his hands over it. He passes his hands over it again and again, and he knows then things that the stonecutter knows and he breaks the stone and seals it and breaks it and seals it and tears at it as if at a cloth. When he has done, he has made a puzzle of the thinnest weave, a puzzle in stone. He puts it beneath his ragged cloak, and goes back to the gates. There he waits until morning, and when the first guard to wake looks out at the sun, he is there.

You again. Have you nothing to sell? Have you the means to buy? The king lifts the cloak to show the stone puzzle, and the guard's eyes follow the impossible lines and turns and corners. Round about they go, round about and around and they fall into nothing, into nowhere. Again he tries, again, he can reach nowhere with the puzzle, with his eyes on the puzzle. Very well, he says. You are welcome to the city, and he opens the gate. The king covers his puzzle, and goes then upon the streets of his own city. Never has he seen it so well. The merchants are opening their stalls in the squares and streets. Animals are being fed, watered, slaughtered, skinned, ground, groomed, their manes tied with ribbons. He finds his familiar way to the castle. There is another gate. I will see the king, he says. Anyone has a right, says the guard, to see the king. But it may be the end of you. The guard brushes the king's hood back and looks upon his face. But he does not see anyone he knows. He has not seen this person before. Good fortune to you, he says, and opens the gate.

Then the king is upon the courtyard of his own castle. He goes along the passages as a claimant, with the others who have things to ask. They are endless in number, it seems, and they are admitted, all at once, to an interior chamber where the king will appear and speak to them. The king himself is astonished. He has never spoken to claimants. He has never seen this room. But an hour passes and another, and a counselor comes out and sits in a high chair. I am the king, he says. I know you, thinks the king. You are but a counselor. And so the king makes himself the last of all those there, and waits, and when they have all spoken to the counselor, and when they have all gone away, he presents himself, saying, I have something to say to the king, but you are not the king. I am not the king, agrees the counselor, stepping down off the high chair, but we will go to him now. So, they go down more hallways and cross more courts, the counselor, the king, and the guards, and they enter another chamber, where another counselor, yet higher, sits. I have known these men all my life, thinks the king, and never did I know . . . but already he is brought forward. Here is the king, they say to him. Tell him what you will. You are not the king, he says. I have come to see the king. And so they draw back the cloth at the back of the room, the heavy, rich, banded cloth, and there is another passage, and they go down it, the king, the first counselor, the second counselor, and the guards, and they reach a place where the guards can go no farther, and the counselors lead the king on, one on each side. His clothes are so filthy, his face so etched with weather and sun, that they can scarcely bear to be beside him, yet they pass on together. Into the final chamber they go. There sits the king, and he knows himself. He has seen that face, so often! To him he goes, and when the king on his throne perceives the stonecutter's robes, when he perceives the stonecutter's hands, when he perceives that the stonecutter has passed all obstacles to come before him, he opens his eyes wide as any owl, and calls out. Who has let this man in? To the counselors, there is a lowly stonecutter, standing before their king. And this is what they see. The king holds out his hands and the stonecutter opens his robe and holds out his impossible puzzle, this fashioning of stone and light. The king receives it into his hands and there he makes it again the stone it was, and he sets it beside him, as it had sat in the field.

Then the king wakes, and it is morning. The lords have saddled their horses. Come, they say, come let us ride away. And the king rouses himself from the table where he was sleeping and he goes to his horse. Out from the hut comes the stonecutter and he looks into the king's face. What passes between them then is neither for lords, nor for storytellers. Who can say what it means to be one person and not another? When they returned to the city, the king did nothing as he had before, and he led his kingdom into a new age, which even now has been forgotten. Of it, we have only this tale.

INT.   You felt before that all things were inevitable, that nothing could be done. But when you read that, you saw that there was a tiller? That things truly could be changed, and even one man could do it?

KAKUZO   Exactly. I felt I could be the stonecutter.

INT.   But there is no king. Even if you could be the stone-cutter, I don't see . . .

KAKUZO   The king is now in general. The kingship is held in general. It is what is tolerated by the people.

INT.   Then, to change their vision, you would need to . . .

KAKUZO   I needed to speak to everyone at once.

INT.   But you were young, and finding your way. How did you make your plans? How did you set them in motion? It was the middle of the 1970s. Perhaps—civil and legal formality was the farthest thing from anyone's mind?

KAKUZO   Not so. There were some of us who were concerned. It seemed that Japan had the chance to become what no other nation was or has been: an actually fair place. I wanted that, more than anything. In my own way, I would say, though I'm sure others would disagree with me, I would say I am . . .

INT.   A moral man? A patriotic man?

KAKUZO   Maybe not in the sense of one who follows the emperor, who gives up everything for someone else's cause. I gave up everything, but for my own cause.

INT.   Did you? Or did you convince Sotatsu to do so on your behalf?

KAKUZO   His life was a zero. He would have done nothing. Instead, look: someone is writing a book about it.

(Laughs, spits on the floor.)

INT.   I don't . . .

KAKUZO   I had returned home from the city. I reconnected with a girl named Jito Joo. We were living together. She had been my girlfriend some years before that, but things hadn't worked out. I left. Anyway, now that I had returned, we had ended up together again. Oda Sotatsu was an old friend. I started to see him. We were all feeling the same way, very restricted, very angry. Joo and I would stay up all night talking about things that we could do to escape, ways that things could change. I had a few friends who had ended up in jail and I was angry about the justice system. I felt we were very far behind the way it worked in other supposedly civilized countries.

INT.   So, that's what hatched the idea of the confession?

KAKUZO   Partially, yes. It was partially that, and partially just anger.

INT.   Did you have any help in preparing the confession?

KAKUZO   A friend from Sakai, I won't say his name, a lawyer. He helped draft it. The intention was that it be legally binding, to a degree. Of course, it is difficult to make it truly binding. But, as binding as we could make it, we did.

INT.   And had you targeted Sotatsu all along? You knew that he would be the one?

KAKUZO   I felt that, and I wasn't alone in this—I felt that I was too important as the organizer to be the one who would be in prison. I didn't see that as my part of the task.

INT.   You saw that as Sotatsu's part?

KAKUZO   He was well suited to it. I knew him to be honorable, to have great inner resources. I also knew that he had obtained a very, I don't know, bleak outlook. He was not very happy at that time, when I had returned. I was unsurprised when he agreed.

INT.   I should tell you that I have been in contact with many different people in my research for this. Among them, the entire Oda family, and Jito Joo.

KAKUZO   Joo also?

INT.   Yes.

KAKUZO   You have to be careful whom you trust. Everyone has a version, and most of them are wrong. In fact, I can tell you clearly: they are all wrong. I am in a position to help you understand what happened. You need to understand, Mr. Ball, the world is made up almost entirely of sentimental fools and brutes.

INT.   And which are you?

KAKUZO   (laughs)

INT.   Truly.

KAKUZO   A sentimental brute, I suppose. One who means well, but has no feeling for others.

[*Int. note.* Here Kakuzo gave me the tape of the initial night—the actual tape of the moment when Sotatsu was lured into confessing. I was shocked. At first, I had trouble believing the truth of it, but when I listened, I knew it could be nothing else. Among the many things that were strange and beautiful, one was the manner in which the voices of Kakuzo and Joo were different from when I had spoken with them, but subtly. It was a weight of time—all the time that had passed since the tape had been made, and all the things that had happened.]

[After handing me the materials, Kakuzo did not want to be interviewed any more. He merely gave me the tape of that first interaction, and a series of statements. The statements I provide hereafter, verbatim (changed only as per my initial note). The statements were of drastically varying age, some even predating the events. I will enumerate them below.]

Statements (*Sato Kakuzo*)

[*Int. note.* The statements were carbon copies of originals that Kakuzo kept. I occasionally had difficulty making out a word here or there. In such cases, I strove to keep meaning clear and chose the least outlandish or strange usage. Some of the statements were little more than scraps. Others were on larger paper, printed with diagrams and explanatory text. I do not give all here, as the relationship of some to the matter at hand was tangential at best.]

1. Narito Disappearances: Blueprint
2. The Invention of a Crime
3. Confessions & The Idea of a Confession
4. Joo & How It Went in Practice

Narito Disappearances: BLUEPRINT

1. The abduction of individuals from their homes
2. The confession of a person
3. The trial of that person
4. The execution of that person
5. The reappearance of the various individuals
6. Public acknowledgment of wrongdoing on the part
   of the governing mechanism

The first should be accomplished in total secrecy. There must be no intervention of law enforcement at this time. It should be easily accomplished, but must require elaborate and long-standing plans, as well as the use of specific resources.

The second must involve either: a. an unbreakable person (dedicated to the cause and understanding it thoroughly); or b. a person who will prove unbreakable based upon arbitrary reasons, reasons of peculiarity, i.e., an eccentric.

The third will proceed naturally, as should the fourth.

The fifth is an artificial event, prompted by the announcement of the fourth.

The sixth may be hoped for, and can be accomplished by the pageantry and spectacle of the fifth, particularly by the directedness of the fifth, and the manner in which it places blame.

The Invention of a Crime

The invention of a crime is a special matter. A crime does not exist, and then it is invented. It is not executed. Never is the crime executed; it is merely invented. It is not carried out, but it appears to have been carried out. This appearance of execution creates the crime in the eyes of the populace who beg for enforcement. The individual who accepts guilt for the crime that never occurred is then caught (or comes forward) and is punished. The punishment, of course, is real. Should the society have sufficient resources to detect that the crime is an invented crime, and marry it with an invented execution, similarly un–carried out, though appearing to have been, then the crime would be un–carried out, would be revealed in its un-carried-out-ness and the criminal released. The system would have proven efficacious in the extreme. The chances of such an event are nil.

The invention of a crime is not the province of the criminal mastermind, as it does not, in its essence, involve any crime at all. The principals, both the victims and the agents, are complicit in the event. Some have said that this is always the case (in nature). We do not accept or make that point here. Here we simply say: all involved in the "invented crime" are a part of an organization created for the purpose of arranging the "invented crime," and all have knowledge of the enterprise in which they are embroiled. The single exception may be (and must be) the confessor, if he be of the second type (spoken of previously).

The action of the crime must be such that it involves tremendous fear on the part of the populace with little reason for that fear. In other words, the fear that is generated must be archetypal, must not be truly causally connected with the crime. The fear must be inspired. Any direct connection between the fear and the event of the crime could serve as an infraction of sorts, and would, at the end of all events, prove to be a true crime, actually punishable.

The organization must have within it members capable of long silence and great discretion. The gathering of such individuals is the principal difficulty that faces any organizer at the founding of such an organization. It is most especially problematic when the ethical problem the organization has been created in order to combat is itself vague and full of complication.

To that end: a discussion of confession.

Confessions & The Idea of a Confession

It is at the heart of our human enterprise, that is to say, at the heart of society, to allow consensus a power it ought not to have.

This is to say, if a man makes a soup, a patently bad soup, and another tastes it on the end of a spoon and says to the first, "This is good soup," the soup then is known as good. It is acknowledged good. It fulfills its purpose as soup. The consensus regarding the soup is that the soup is good. It perhaps will be made again in the same way. Others arriving on the scene, perhaps with doubt in their hearts as to their ability to accurately judge a soup to be good or not, they hear this verdict of the soup. They taste the soup and know it to be good. They are not judging the soup themselves; this power they have not obtained: rather they listen to that initial agreement.

When a man has committed a crime, it should be prosecuted in a fair society only if the evidence of that crime may be seen. No imaginary documents, that is to say, documents that are the province solely of the human mind unconnected with the world, should be used toward a prosecution or conviction.

> That we as humans believe we see things
>   we do not see.
> That we will stake our lives and reputations
>   on the above.
> That we as humans believe we have done things
>   we have not.

That we will stake our lives and reputations
on that, too.

Ladies and gentlemen, it is clear that the mechanism of the
law cannot discover all ends. They cannot find all evidence.
It is the nature of the world that all evidence is ground into
nothing, sometimes in mere minutes. It is the nature of the
world that this grinding of evidence into nothing does not
proceed (always) with malice or intention. The world simply renews itself. Chaos and order rear their alternate heads
as two winds that tear at each other's cheeks.

This being the case, it was soon determined (early in the
course of law) that an element, a freeing element, might be
obtained in the search for justice. This freeing element may
be divided into two parts:

1. The first: eyewitness testimony.
2. The second: the confession.

That a person saw something, himself or herself, has long
been accounted a part of the judicial process, however,
it never was given the pride of place that it enjoys today,
principally because the opinion of any one individual was
never accorded respect on the basis of an individual being
an individual. This is to say, in previous times, one's office
as a human did not accord one the full opportunity to both
claim something and be its proof.

In previous times, such proofs were made thusly: by appeal
to the gods.

That agency was then made known through various trials:
trial by combat, trial by fire, trial by water. This then was the

proof. The proof was not the accusation, nor the statement of an individual.

That said, it has generally always been the case that a person willing to confess to a crime may be acknowledged to have performed that crime. Such a position is mistaken: one cannot know that a person has the truth of a thing, most particularly in the manner in which he/she is affected by it. Our knowledge about ourselves is our least reliable knowledge. Yet, so thoroughly do we ordinarily champion our own cause that it is acknowledged *effective* to believe that a person who deems it impossible to any further champion his/her own cause must be guilty. Else, why would he/she not continue to declare innocence?

It is primarily through a judgment that favors efficiency over truth that confessions are deemed viable.

All true convictions should proceed from a scientific investigation the results of which can be replicated (and which should be shown to be replicable). A particular person should not necessarily have any involvement whatsoever in the investigation into or trial of their offense. The world itself should provide all details and all evidence. If such evidence is lacking, then a crime cannot be proven without a doubt, and a person ought not to be convicted or punished.

Joo & How It Went in Practice

[*Int. note.* This was the most recent of the papers. In my opinion, the previous sheets were old notes, written by Sato Kakuzo prior to the Narito Disappearances, likely even prior to his departure from Sakai. This paper, on the other hand, might even have been written in the year I received it, or thereabouts, long after the last gasps of the Narito Disappearances had been forgotten. He begins this with a vague ascription of date, but whether it can be trusted is unclear.]

The Unwilling Participation of Jito Joo

I write now to explain the unwilling participation of Jito Joo in the events of last year. Whether this document will be read by anyone during my life, whether it will be destroyed before anyone has seen it, whether it will be seen next week after I am carted away on some unrelated charge, who can say? I write it in order to not be a part of any deception related to Jito Joo, in order to say my piece about the truth of the matter.

I had known Jito Joo before I returned from Sakai. When we resumed our relationship, it was not much of a surprise to either of us. Things had gone well before I left; they went well after. It was simply a geographical dislocation that made us stop seeing each other. It was a geographical reuniting that prompted the resumption of our relationship.

I will say this also: Joo was smarter, sharper, and more clever than any of the other girls I knew, whether in Sakai or anywhere in Osaka. This alone was a determinant for me. I loathe to repeat myself, and with Joo, one never must. We also shared certain sympathies of temperament, and of political viewpoint. As I see it, the politics of our daily life are inextricable from the larger politics of the world. Therefore, when we felt ourselves confined, when Joo and I, sitting in our small apartment, felt ourselves confined, we sought for ways out.

I had been reading a great deal. I had read of various French attempts to throw off this oppressive air that infiltrates daily life. Debord, Vaneigem, and others had made many attempts, both to inspire, and to act in their own right. This led directly, as I will explain, to the events that I caused, that I and Jito Joo caused, in Osaka Prefecture.

I had planned the matter already. I had a sense of what I wanted to do. My eye had pinpointed a term, had seen a specific, which I felt should be overloaded and made to destroy itself. That specific, that element, was *the confession*. I felt that no one had stood against it sufficiently. I felt that its innate duplicity, its essential divergence from truth or fact, should be marked and seen by all for what it was. Yet wherever I went, whomever I spoke to, I was astonished. The matter was not clear; this matter, so clear to me, was not clear to others. Patently, I saw this as an opportunity, one to be prosecuted with swiftness, if I may take liberties with the phrase.

So, to return to the narrative, I was living there with Joo. I had made a plan, but had no helpers. I was working at the docks, traveling to the docks to work, and returning exhausted. I was angry. I was in love. I was also afraid—I was not sure that Joo would share my adherence to the precise elements of my plan, and once I confided it to her, it would have to go forward in that exact way, else fail.

That is why I trapped her. That is why the first contract was not the contract signed by Oda Sotatsu. The first contract, made in the same way, after a supposed game of chance, was signed by Jito Joo. I was ashamed to have had to make it, ashamed to have had to perpetrate it. But, in the course of time I saw that she would never have agreed to the repeatedly heartless actions that were required of her, had she not been forced by her agreement, and by her fealty to what she saw as her honor.

Joo & How It Went in Practice 2

One night, Joo and I were playing at a game, a game of chance, a comparison of cards, a drawing and comparison of cards. Neither would win more than the other. She would at times win; I would at times win. Our method at first had been to play for forfeits. When the burden of inventing forfeits proved too much, we moved to agreed-upon and more dangerous consequences. We began to cut ourselves with a knife upon a loss. I stepped from a second-story window and injured my leg. She stepped in front of a car and caused it to drive off the road. I give these examples as evidence of the state of mind in which we were going forward. We were in love with each other. We were in love with the mechanism we were using to repel the dank pressure of conformity. We were despairing all the while, because after each arch of our backs, the weight pressed down again, just as strongly as it had before.

Yet, I had my plan. Joo knew nothing of it. I said to her, I said, *Joo, this time we shall write an agreement. We shall make a contract. The contract will bind one to the will of the other for a period of time.* She objected. A period of time? How banal. Why not the course of a project, why not for the duration of some project, that therefore could stand for a week or a year or more. This was the sort of thing Joo would suggest. I agreed, and so we hammered out the terms of the bargain. The loser would be forced to obey the other entirely within the confines of the proceeding, of the particular project. Beyond that, he or she could have his/her will, but only insomuch as he/she would not affect the successful execution of the project by his/her actions.

I wrote it up. We cosigned the establishment of a bargain: that the loser of our card game would be forced to sign the sheet. We dated it.

We then sat facing each other. I laid the cards out. She cut them and drew one. I cut them and drew another. I won and she signed the agreement. It was as simple as that. I had placed the cards in order, and knew where to look for my winning card. She didn't guess that I would do such a thing. She didn't realize that there was a thing for which I was working, a thing for which I would cheat. But there was, and I did. And from then on, I had Jito Joo's complete obedience in all matters related to the Narito Disappearances.

She never went back on her agreement, and she never threatened to. She never wanted to see it. Indeed, I did not keep it. I destroyed it immediately, the very day she signed it. To see such a document, and remember my behavior in relation to it—I wanted no part of that. I was looking to the future. I was thinking on how I could use her, and how I could cause a dislocation in the life of my society.

How It Went in Practice

As you may now suspect, the matter of the card game, as played with Oda Sotatsu, was similarly rotten. Joo and I got him to the bar; we got him drunk. Joo flirted with him. I complimented him. He was a man in a difficult situation. His life was difficult, bleak. He had little, and little to look forward to. In this way he was entirely typical, yet he was not typical in his nature. In his nature, he was proud, he was unrelenting. I knew what I had in Oda Sotatsu.

That he lost the card game, that he signed the confession: it was all inevitable. I had created the situation in my mind while sitting in a room in Sakai, a year before. I had moved shapes, edged like paper, in the stanzas of my head, and now I was watching as Sotatsu wrote on a sheet of paper. He wrote, Oda Sotatsu, and wrote the date, and he looked up at me, and I was looking at him from far away. I knew then that I had done it.

He left the bar, went away, it didn't matter where. The farther the better. If they had had to hunt for him, it wouldn't have changed a thing. I took Joo by the arm, I went home with her. We slept together. I read the confession like a poet reads a poem he has written, a poem which he feels will change his fortunes. But like a poet, it is not his own fortune that his poems change.

How It Went in Practice 2

I had noticed that Sotatsu was watching Joo, was looking at her. I knew her to be what she was—not only pretty, not only a pretty girl, a girl one wanted, but also a smart girl, a girl whose opinion was worthwhile. She would say sharp things and make people look stupid. She had, in fact, done this to Sotatsu. She had done it to me. Shall I say, most of the other girls we had ever met weren't like that? I knew Sotatsu thought much of her, and so the thought crept into my mind, as I lay there, knowing that elsewhere in the town, Sotatsu lay, awaiting the arrival of the police, the thought crept in: should I send her to him? Could Jito Joo be the method for holding Sotatsu to his pledge? I looked at her where she lay naked beside me, and I felt completely sure. I felt not only that it would work, but that she would do it. Despite the fact that she need not do it, that she could claim it went beyond anything agreed to, it remained true. Our very helplessness in the face of our lives, the fact that we wanted to be drastic, and that we wanted to force that drasticness on others—it meant she would throw herself willingly off this cliff. She would let me tell her to go to him, and she would go to him, and she would hold him to his pledge.

Joo, I said, when I woke her, *take this confession.*

She stood and dressed while I watched her, and I thought, this is the essence of my life—not before or after will I have so many fine things at such fullness: the love of a girl, the plight of a friend, the grand opening of a conspiracy. I felt it all. And now, later, I can tell you—I was not wrong. There has been nothing to compare that moment to, and I expect there will not be. I expect very little now.

How It Went in Practice 3

If I am explaining how it went, I should explain it all, I guess. Friends in Sakai had an uncle. He owned a farm. He was a hateful man. The farm was an old place, etched out of a hillside. Nothing was near it, just a mostly abandoned shrine. He wasn't even a very good farmer. The sort of man who could live on sawdust, who perhaps was made of sawdust. I met him; I traveled there with the express purpose of meeting him. I met him, and we got along well. He was a converted anarchist. He was an anarchist in a non-political sense. He was a sort of poverty-stricken miscreant who didn't at all have a bad time of it. He enjoyed sitting outside in the morning time, and that was about it. I won him over by confessing how much I hated people. This surprised him: you hate people too? Yes, I do. I hate people. Well, we have that in common, then. So, we sat together in the morning time, and I described to him this fantastic plot I had come up with. It was a huge insult, I told him, we were throwing a huge insult in the face of the society. They would have to bear it. There was no way they could do anything else but bear it. He found the whole thing very funny. He agreed.

And so it became my lot: to travel in a borrowed car from place to place, finding old people with odd views, and convincing them, *Go away for a while. I have a place for you.*

In my defense, I explained the whole thing to each one. I explained to each one what it was that I was doing. I told them they might have to stay away for a year or two, or three, for five years even, ten. Who could say? I spoke for a long time, a very long time, and I did it again and again and again. In every case, when I had finished, the person got up, leaving everything just as it was. In every case, when I had finished, the person got up, and we walked out to the car. We got into the car, and we drove away.

One by one, I drove each person to the farm, where the old man took them in. There they lived together, a little boardinghouse of the oddest folk you've ever seen. The funny thing is, they got along very well together. I believe the time when they were disappeared was the happiest time most of those people had seen in many years.

When I'd driven the last one there, I didn't go back, not until the whole thing was over. I didn't even send a message. That was part of the bargain. I'd explained it all to the old man. I'd explained it to each of them. We were all of one mind.

How It Went in Practice 4

Joo fell into it. I didn't know it would go that way. She fell into it like an actress. You would never have known she didn't care at all about Sotatsu. I said to her sometimes, *Joo, Joo*. I shook her, I woke her up, I said, *Joo, go there, visit him now. You have to keep it up.* She'd say, no, no. She'd curl into me, into the blankets. I want to stay here, she'd say. But, I would push her off. I'd pull off the blanket. She'd stand up, shake herself off. Go on, I'd say. She would nod, and change, and go off. Remember, I would tell her, as she looked back at me: I don't exist. Nothing exists except Sotatsu's resolve. Make him know it. Make him know he can hold out.

For the most part, it went well. There was trouble when Sotatsu's brother came, but Joo fixed it. She was quick. I told you she was. She undid whatever the brother did. She kept Sotatsu to himself, to his own resolve, to what he had decided. I couldn't have imagined a better handler. She got so I didn't even have to tell her to go. She would just go on her own. I would wake up and she would be gone. Then I'd be working, I'd take a breath during the day and think:

There on the farm, my disappeared people are standing in a line, looking down the mountain. There in the prison, Sotatsu is standing, looking at the wall. There in the bus, Jito Joo is sitting, looking at her feet. I am no one. No one knows that I am anyone, but my plan is inevitable. The judges are doing what I am telling them to do, simply because I understand better than they do this one thing: the absurd lengths to which human beings go to prove themselves reasonable.

How It Went in Practice 5

I was worried often. I can't pretend I didn't wake in a sweat most nights, afraid that something had gone wrong. Sometimes Joo would tease me, too. She'd arrive crying, saying he had recanted, he had confessed, only to break into laughter when she saw my horrified face. It's not a joke, I would tell her, and she would laugh. Joo, Joo, I would say. You are a hard one.

But when the sentence had gone through, and when he was on death row, I felt more secure. That much, at least, had been secured. I was afraid too that some of my disappeared people would die. They were old! People die sometimes—yet it would not be easy to account for. I had nothing to do but wait, and I could not even learn how things were at the farm.

Several months into his stay on death row, Sotatsu started behaving strangely. He started writing odd things on paper. He started talking to the guards. I was worried that he was breaking down. That's when I told Joo: I wanted her to go there and sleep with him, if it could be managed. I wanted her to bind him to her that way.

She broke into tears. She didn't want to. I said you have to. You don't have any choice. She said she wouldn't do it. I said you will. You need to. She got her things and went out. She never came back. Whether she did go or not, to the prison, I can't say. I never saw her again.

The next day, I heard the news on the radio.

FIN

+

One day in the springtime, when I was still a child, Oda Sotatsu was taken from his prison cell. He was led down hallways. He was asked to show that he was indeed himself, and he showed it. Others agreed to it. He was led into one room after another, past statues. He was made to stand on a flat trapdoor and when the word was given he was hanged by the neck until dead.

The news was broadcast by radio and by television to the general population. There was happiness, but also confusion. Many there were who wanted to know—what had happened to the disappeared.

Then, one week following the execution, in the city of Sakai, a procession appeared in the street. It was a procession of people dressed all in white, every one, and led by a young man, Sato Kakuzo. They were dressed as penitents, in the old fashion, he and all those who were supposedly disappeared, those for whose sake Oda Sotatsu had been executed. They were still living, and they walked in a procession through the streets to the courthouse, while the city looked on in astonishment. There on the steps of the courthouse, Sato Kakuzo delivered a speech to members of the press and a crowd that had gathered, following the procession. In his speech he accused the society of the crime it had committed, making it known that the murder of the innocent man Oda Sotatsu had gone forward, and that others too, in the days and years to come, would be executed, on no evidence at all.

We cannot allow this, he said. *Those of you still living, those of us still living, we cannot allow this. If you live still, with your actions declare, we cannot allow this.*

The newspapers printed the matter.

Some weeks passed, and it was essentially forgotten. When I learned of it, I felt I should write about it. I felt it must have been written about. I felt there must have been books and books about it. There were none. I felt my life and my experience, my loss suited me to the task, so I set this down, this book.

This then is the book about it. This is the record of Oda Sotatsu and his life, and of the plot of Sato Kakuzo, and of the love of Jito Joo.

Acknowledgments

Here acknowledge for generosity in the execution of appointed and unappointed tasks of every conceivable kind:

NYC
J. Jackson & all at Vintage, Pantheon, Random House.
Billy, David, Becky, Jessie & all at Kuhn Projects.

ELSEWHERE
C. Ball, Th. Bjornsdottir, A. Aegisdottir.

CHICAGO
Salazar Larus, Nora, Nutmeg & Skunkur Amelius.
S. Levine, L. Wainwright, J. McManus, J. Francis, R. Inoue.

ABOUT THE AUTHOR

Jesse Ball is the author of three previous novels, including *Samedi the Deafness,* and several works of verse, bestiaries, and sketchbooks. His prizes include the 2008 *Paris Review* Plimpton Prize; his verse has been included in the Best American Poetry series. He gives classes on lucid dreaming and lying at the School of the Art Institute of Chicago.

A NOTE ON THE TYPE

This book was set in Albertina, the best known of the typefaces designed by Chris Brand (b. 1921 in Utrecht, the Netherlands). Issued by the Monotype Corporation in 1965, Albertina was one of the first text fonts made solely for photocomposition. It was first used to catalog the work of Stanley Morison and was exhibited in Brussels at the Albertina Library in 1966.

Composed by North Market Street Graphics, Lancaster, Pennsylvania

Printed and bound by Berryville Graphics, Berryville, Virginia

Designed by Maggie Hinders